LAST RIDE

Longarm's bullet drove into the horse's chest. He hated like the devil to shoot a good horse, but he didn't figure he had any choice. He wanted to capture the sombrero-wearing bushwhacker, not kill him.

The mortally wounded horse's front legs folded up underneath it, sending the animal crashing to the earth. The bushwhacker sailed through the air, landed hard and rolled a couple of times. He came up groggily, struggling to his feet, but by the time he made it, Longarm was on top of him. Longarm lashed out with the Henry rifle. The barrel thudded against the man's head, his knees unhinged, and he fell stunned to the ground . . .

TABOR EVANS

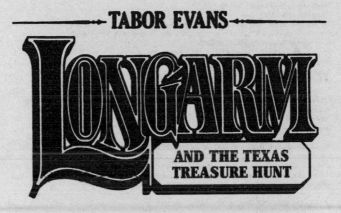

LONGARM

AND THE TEXAS TREASURE HUNT

JOVE BOOKS, NEW YORK

THE BERKLEY PUBLISHING GROUP
Published by the Penguin Group
Penguin Group (USA) Inc.
375 Hudson Street, New York, New York 10014, USA
Penguin Group (Canada), 10 Alcorn Avenue, Toronto, Ontario M4V 3B2, Canada
(a division of Pearson Penguin Canada Inc.)
Penguin Books Ltd., 80 Strand, London WC2R 0RL, England
Penguin Group Ireland, 25 St. Stephen's Green, Dublin 2, Ireland (a division of Penguin Books Ltd.)
Penguin Group (Australia), 250 Camberwell Road, Camberwell, Victoria 3124, Australia
(a division of Pearson Australia Group Pty. Ltd.)
Penguin Books India Pvt. Ltd., 11 Community Centre, Panchsheel Park, New Delhi—110 017, India
Penguin Group (NZ), Cnr. Airborne and Rosedale Roads, Albany, Auckland 1310, New Zealand
(a division of Pearson New Zealand Ltd.)
Penguin Books (South Africa) (Pty.) Ltd., 24 Sturdee Avenue, Rosebank, Johannesburg 2196,
South Africa

Penguin Books Ltd., Registered Offices: 80 Strand, London WC2R 0RL, England

This is a work of fiction. Names, characters, places, and incidents either are the product of the author's imagination or are used fictitiously, and any resemblance to actual persons, living or dead, business establishments, events, or locales is entirely coincidental.

LONGARM AND THE TEXAS TREASURE HUNT

A Jove Book / published by arrangement with the author

PRINTING HISTORY
Jove edition / July 2005

Copyright © 2005 by The Berkley Publishing Group

ISBN: 0-515-13966-1

JOVE®
Jove Books are published by The Berkley Publishing Group,
a division of Penguin Group (USA) Inc.,
375 Hudson Street, New York, New York 10014.
JOVE is a registered trademark of Penguin Group (USA) Inc.
The "J" design is a trademark belonging to Penguin Group (USA) Inc.

PRINTED IN THE UNITED STATES OF AMERICA

10   9   8   7   6   5   4   3   2   1

Chapter 1

It was just whore talk, Millie Ames thought, the sort of babbling that a man did when he had paid a woman to go to bed with him and was nervous about it for one reason or another. Millie had been a soiled dove for two years and knew that some men would go on and on about anything and everything. A lot of them even talked about their wives, which always struck her as odd. Why would a fella want to yammer about his wife while he was screwin' another woman? It didn't make sense.

Then the old-timer started talking about money, and Millie's interest perked right up.

He wasn't talking about the money it had cost him to bring her upstairs to the little room on the second floor of the saloon. She had already collected that. Instead, as he sat down on the edge of the bed in his long underwear and started to take off his boots, he said, "You know what they do with old money?"

She thought for a second that it was a joke or a riddle or something like that, but he seemed really interested in hearing her answer. She had already taken off her short, spangled dress. Now she peeled off the shift she wore under it and stood there in front of him clad only in silk

1

stockings and a narrow black ribbon tied around her neck. She liked the way the ribbon looked.

"I don't have any idea," she said as she raised her arms and ran her fingers through her long red hair. She knew the gesture lifted her breasts and made them more prominent. She saw the old-timer swallow as he stared at the firm globes riding high on her chest. "What do you mean, old money?"

"Bills that've been in circulation a long time. They sometimes get torn up a mite, and stained, and sorta ratty. Folks don't want money like that."

"I figure as long as it spends, there's nothing wrong with it." Millie stretched and thrust her red-furred pelvis forward a little. That drew the old man's attention, too. He licked his lips.

"Yeah, I reckon I feel the same way. But when somebody brings some o' that old money into a bank, the teller sets it aside, so that it gets took outta circulation."

Despite her habit of getting her customers worked up as quickly as possible, so that they didn't waste much of her valuable time, Millie found herself getting more interested.

"You mean they just get rid of it, even though it's still good money?"

"Yeah, when the bank's got a big enough pile of bills set aside, they send 'em to a bigger bank, and when that bank's got a big enough stash, they ship all them old bills back to the mint and get 'em replaced with new money. The gov'-ment only keeps a certain amount o' cash circulatin' at one time, so they got to take some in when they let some out."

Millie saw the bulge in his drawers and felt a little tingle of satisfaction. She had thought for a second she was losing her natural talent for making men randy. She sat down on the bed beside the old-timer and leaned closer to him to kiss him as she reached down and caressed his erection. She wasn't sure how old he was. His hair and beard were all white, and his skin was weathered and browned by years of exposure to the elements.

2

From the feel of it through his underwear, though, he had a nice one, and she'd gotten it hard without any trouble. As she kissed him she took one of his hands and brought it to her breasts. Even though she didn't get much pleasure out of this stuff except with Salado, she did like having her nipples played with.

She wanted to get on with it, but then her curiosity got the better of her. She pulled back a little and asked, "So what happens to all the old money once it goes back to the government?"

"They burn it up. Millions o' dollars up in smoke."

Millie frowned. "That just doesn't seem right. There ought to be something they could do with it."

The old-timer chuckled and said, "Like give it to some deservin' folks?"

"Well, yeah, I guess."

"That's what me an' my partners thought. Only we knew the gov'ment wouldn't never give it to us, so we decided to just take it."

Millie's frown deepened. "What are you talking about?"

The old man laughed again and squeezed the breast he was holding a little harder as he became more animated. "We took it right off'n the train that was carryin' it back to Denver. No tellin' how much all them old bills came to. Hundreds o' thousands for sure. Maybe as much as a million."

"The Cottonwood Station holdup," Millie breathed.

The old-timer looked surprised. "You heard of it?"

"Of course. It was one of the most famous train robberies ever. When the law never caught up to the robbers or found the money, people said Jesse James must've been behind it."

"Jesse James!" the old man said with a snort. "I reckon ol' Jesse was a pretty good holdup man in his day, but he never pulled a job like me an' my pards did. That was the most loot anybody ever snatched off a train."

3

Millie glanced at the patched, worn range clothes and the battered, shapeless hat that the old-timer had taken off and dropped in a corner. That wasn't the outfit of a rich man. And the hand still kneading her breast wasn't the hand of a rich man, either, not with those calluses and gnarled fingers.

"What's your name?" she asked.

"Claude Farley. That's my legal moniker, too. It ain't no alias."

"I never heard of any famous outlaw named Claude Farley."

"You don't believe me?" He sounded offended.

"Now, don't get your back up, old-timer. It's just that you don't look like a fella who stole a million dollars off a train."

"Look like an old saddle tramp, do I?"

"Well . . ."

He sighed and let his hands dangle between his knees. What he and Millie had been about to do was forgotten for the moment.

"You're right. I *am* an old saddle tramp. But it ain't my fault. The sumbitch who planned the whole thing double-crossed me an' my other partner. He disappeared with all the loot 'fore we could split it up. We took just as many risks as he did, but we was left with nothin'." Claude Farley's twisted hands clenched into fists. "Ten years! Ten years I been lookin' for that bastard . . . and now I found him!"

Millie's green eyes widened. "What? You know where he is?"

"Damn right I do. Luck was finally with me. And as soon as I get to Buffalo Flat, I'm gonna be a rich man." He grinned over at Millie. "You wanna go with me, honey? If you're gonna be a whore, you might as well be doin' it with a rich man as a poor one!"

That made sense to Millie. She'd wanted to shake off the dust of this Kansas cowtown ever since she'd lit down here and gone to whoring. Maybe now she could, and if she treated this old man right, he might be plenty generous with her. She reached for his groin again.

"Hold on there," Farley said. "How'd a gal like you ever hear about that Cottonwood Station holdup? You must've been just a younker when it happened."

"I was nine," Millie said. "My folks were dead, and I lived with my aunt and uncle. He was a sheriff, so I heard a lot about robberies and such."

Farley nodded. "Oh. I reckon that makes sense. Go ahead with what you was doin'."

Deftly, she unbuttoned the long underwear and freed his shaft. It was a nice one, all right, and she decided to give it a little special treatment. She leaned over and took the head in her mouth.

Memories tried to crowd in on her brain. She had been nine at the time of the Cottonwood Station holdup. Three years later, when she was twelve, her uncle the sheriff, that respected pillar of the community, had come to her bed in the middle of the night and put his cock in her mouth for the first time. But not the last time, oh, no. Hell, no.

He'd been considerate, by his lights. He'd waited until she was thirteen before he actually raped her.

Millie forced those thoughts out of her head. She had put up with all that stuff for four more years, but finally she'd had enough and had run away from the little town in Iowa. All the bad things were behind her. Well, being a whore wasn't the best life in the world, she supposed, but at least she was getting paid for it now, and it wasn't her own flesh and blood doing it to her.

And maybe luck was finally smiling on her. Claude Farley had picked her to take upstairs, and he had told her about the fortune in old greenbacks and how he was finally going to get his hands on the money again.

Damn right she'd go with him. She would miss Salado, more than likely, but enough cash would soften the blow of losing him.

Farley rested a hand on her head as she continued the French lesson for several minutes. He moaned and grunted and seemed to be thoroughly enjoying himself. Finally, though, he said, "You better hold off there, gal. I want to finish this off good an' proper."

Millie lifted her head and tossed back some of the long, straight red hair that had fallen over her face. She scooted back on the narrow bed and reclined, spreading her thighs as she did so. She knew she looked lovely in the candlelight that washed over her body; enough men had told her so over the past two years. The hair between her legs was thick and a slightly darker red than that on her head. It framed the pink cleft of her sex.

Farley stood up and pushed the bottom half of his long underwear down over his scrawny hips and legs. He kicked them off and climbed onto the bed. Millie smiled and opened her legs a little more in invitation. Farley crawled into position and poised the head of his shaft against her opening.

"Lord, gal, I don't think I been this hard in years," he said. "What's your name?"

"Millie. And that's my real name, too."

"Well, Millie, I'm gonna give you a good hard ride. You ready?"

She nodded. "Give it to me good, big fella."

As soon as the words were out of her mouth, she felt a little embarrassed by them. That really was whore talk, the sort of thing a soiled dove said to every customer, even the ones who weren't big down there at all. She wanted it to be different with Claude Farley. Eventually, if she stayed with him and played her cards right, he might not even think of her as a whore anymore. He might even—did she dare think it?—ask her to marry him someday. She had heard stories about whores who married rich customers, but she had never actually known any.

Thankfully, Farley didn't seem to notice. He just shoved it in her and went to pumping.

Millie put her arms around his neck, hung on, and closed her eyes. She had learned a long time ago, with her uncle, in fact, that it was easier that way. The motions were all practiced by now so that she didn't have to think about them. She could let her mind drift to wherever it wanted to go.

Tonight it suddenly warned her that she was placing an awful lot of faith in what this old-timer had told her. What if he was lying? Men *had* been known to lie to women before, she told herself. Maybe there wasn't any money. Maybe he had just heard of the Cottonwood Station robbery and hadn't had anything to do with it. He was getting on in years, after all, and there wasn't much about him to impress a woman, even a soiled dove. It was natural for a man to want a woman he was going to bed with to think highly of him, even when he was paying for the privilege. Maybe, she thought bleakly, she had gotten all her hopes up for nothing.

But he had sounded so sincere, and he had seemed so positive that all he had to do was get to Buffalo Flat, wherever that was, in order to be rich. Surely it was worth a chance. She had only been in this business for two years, Millie thought. She could still put it behind her. If she didn't, she was going to wind up like the other girls, old and worn-out before their time, some of them riddled with disease. And when you took scores of strange men to your bed, there was always the risk that one of them would turn out to be addled in the head and might choke you or stab you or something. Millie had heard about things like that happening, too.

She would take the chance, she decided. She would go with Farley to Buffalo Flat. Shoot, if worse came to worst, she was sure there were plenty of randy men there, too.

Farley was still huffing and puffing and pounding away

7

at her. She wasn't sure how much time had passed while she was thinking, but it seemed like he ought to be done by now. He was old, though, she reminded herself. Fellas like that needed more time. Sometimes they couldn't even finish off at all, no matter what she did.

But then Farley thrust himself into her again and his organ swelled even more and began to spasm. Out of habit, she said, "Yes, Claude, yes!" like she was climaxing, too, and he jerked a couple of times as he finished. Then he slumped limply on top of her, his head banging into her shoulder.

Poor old fart. She had really taken it out of him.

Millie lay there for a moment, breathing a little hard from exertion, not excitement, although the thought of all that loot did sort of arouse her. Farley didn't say anything. He seemed to be getting heavier. She pushed at his shoulder.

"Claude, honey, you got to get up now. Claude? Darlin'?"

Millie pushed harder on his shoulder and tried to scoot out from under him. His head lolled to the side so that she could see his face.

She looked in disbelief into his wide, staring, lifeless eyes for about ten seconds before she started to scream.

Chapter 2

Salado Kyle didn't look much like a gambler. With his tall, slender body and his open, innocent face, he looked more like a choir boy who had somehow wandered into the saloon and found himself in the middle of a poker game. The men who played against him seldom realized until it was too late that he had had plenty of experience with the pasteboards.

And he was so slick hardly anybody ever figured out that he was cheating. The few times it had happened, there had been gunplay, but Salado was slick there, too, and had managed to plug the other fellas before they plugged him. Of course, that meant lighting a shuck out of whatever town he happened to be in at the time, but he never cared about that. He'd been a rootless wanderer ever since he had departed his hometown of Salado, Texas, several years earlier, one jump ahead of a mob that would have gladly helped him leave town—riding on a rail and wearing a coat of tar and feathers.

It had been a lonely existence most of the time, he would have admitted if somebody had held a gun to his head and forced him to look deeply into the previously unknown territory of his heart. Until, that is, he had met Millie Ames.

Falling in love was a damned stupid thing to do, especially if you were a gambler and the gal was a whore, neither of which professions lent itself to stability and permanence. But try telling that to two young people besotted with each other.

The way he felt about Millie was why he completely forgot about the money on the table in front of him when he heard the scream from upstairs. That was her voice, Salado thought as he sprang up from his chair and dropped his cards on the green felt of the poker table. He turned and ran toward the stairs, ignoring the startled yells from the other players in the game.

Salado carried a Smith & Wesson .38 pocket revolver, the model known as the Baby Russian, in a holster under his left arm. He reached under his coat and drew the gun as he leaped up the stairs, taking them two and three at a time. The screaming stopped when he was halfway to the second floor. He didn't know if that was a good sign or a bad one. When he reached the landing he grabbed the railing with his free hand and flung himself toward the door of Millie's room.

He should have put his foot down, he thought wildly. He should have told her no more whoring. It wasn't that the idea of all those men bedding the woman he loved bothered him all that much; he had never believed that fidelity was a workable concept. Whoring was dangerous, though.

But it was her choice as a line of work, and if he had told her to stop, she might have told him to stop cheating at cards, which was probably even more dangerous, and Salado knew that wasn't going to happen. So each of them had just gone along and hoped for the best.

If something had happened to her, he would never forgive himself. Never.

He burst into her room, the Baby Russian cocked and ready in his hand. He swung the barrel wildly from side to side as he looked for something to shoot at in the flickering candlelight.

"Damn it, Salado, don't shoot!" Millie cried.

His jackrabbiting gaze lit on the bed. At first he didn't see her, just the pale, scrawny rear end of the old man who had taken her upstairs. Then he saw the wideflung legs on either side of that elderly rump and realized that Millie was still underneath the old-timer. He caught a glimpse of her eyes peering at him over the old man's shoulder.

"What's wrong?" he asked, confused. She had brought the old man up here to go to bed with him, hadn't she? From the looks of things, that goal had been accomplished.

"Get him off of me, you damn fool! He's dead!"

Salado's jaw and the gun in his hand both sagged toward the floor. "Dead?" he repeated.

"As a doornail," Millie snapped. "Give me a hand here, Salado. It's gettin' hard to breathe." Her eyes narrowed in anger as she saw the grin tugging at his mouth. "Don't you dare laugh at me, damn you! This is serious business!"

"What did you do?" Salado asked as he carefully lowered the hammer of the Smith & Wesson and slipped it back into its holster under his arm. "Screw him to death? Wait a minute—that appears to be exactly what happened!"

"Shut . . . up!" she hissed. "Just shut up and get him off me."

Trying not to smile, Salado heeled the door shut behind him and went across the room to the bed. He didn't have to go far, since whores' quarters were not noted for their spaciousness. He reached down and got hold of the old man's upper left arm, feeling a little surge of revulsion as he felt how slack and lifeless it was. He had touched dead bodies before—how else were you going to search their pockets?—but he had never cared for it.

With a grunt of effort, he rolled the deceased old-timer off of Millie. "He's heavier than he looks."

11

"Why do you think I couldn't budge him?" she asked as she sat up and swung her stocking-clad legs off the bed. A little shiver went through her. "That's the first time that ever happened to me."

"Should I start worrying when we do it? I think my heart's in pretty good shape, but obviously going to bed with you is dangerous—"

She punched him in the belly.

Millie was a tall girl, almost as tall as Salado, and she was no shrinking violet. The punch packed enough power so that he went "Oooff!" and bent over, holding his stomach. For a moment he couldn't seem to get his breath, and when he could, he raised his head and demanded angrily, "What the hell was that for?"

"So you'll listen to me and really pay attention." Millie caught hold of his shirt and pulled him closer to her. "Before he died, that old man told me he was going to be rich."

Salado shook his head in disgust. "What, he found some gold mine or something? The lost treasure of the San Saba?"

"I don't know anything about that. He said he was part of the gang that pulled the Cottonwood Station holdup."

Salado shook his head again, this time in ignorance. "I don't know what you're talking about."

Millie let go of him and rolled her eyes as she started to pull her clothes on hurriedly. She said, "It was a famous train robbery. I heard about it when I was a girl. Three men took over a little train station in eastern Colorado and stopped a train that was carrying hundreds of thousands of dollars, maybe as much as a million. I didn't know it at the time, but it was all old currency on its way back to Denver to be destroyed."

"And that old saddle tramp claimed to be one of the robbers?"

"That's right. He said he never got his share of the loot because the boss of the gang double-crossed him and the other man. But Claude had found out where the double-crosser was now and planned to go there and settle up."

"Not that I believe a word of this," Salado said, "but where's this mysterious mastermind supposed to be hidden?"

"In some place called Buffalo Flat."

For the first time, Salado felt a tickle of real interest. "Buffalo Flat, Texas?"

"I don't know. He just said Buffalo Flat. After that he didn't talk much, if you know what I mean, and then he . . . he . . ."

Suddenly, surprisingly, tears began to well from Millie's eyes. She tried to wipe them away, but Salado saw them and went to her, resting his hands on her shoulders.

"He was just an old man, Millie," he said quietly. "It was his time to go. His heart gave out. You can tell that by looking at him. I'd be willing to bet that he died happy, too. I say that as a professional gambler who knows how to figure the odds on things."

Millie sniffled and managed to smile a little. "I know. I just . . . When you do the things that I do, you can't help but get a little close to the men . . . I just never had somebody *die* on me like that!"

"It's all right," Salado soothed her. "You're sure he didn't say Buffalo Flat, Texas?"

She gave an exasperated sigh. "Why's it so important now?

He's dead! He won't ever go there to claim his share of the loot."

"No," Salado said, "but somebody else could."

Millie's eyes got big again, and she said softly, "Oh, my Lord."

"I've never heard of a settlement called Buffalo Flat anywhere except the one in Texas. I know where it is, but I've never been there. I reckon I could find it, though."

Visible excitement gripped her. "How would we know where to look for the money?"

"Well, we wouldn't. We'd just have to start out by snooping around some. How long ago did you say that robbery was?"

"Ten years."

"We'd start by finding out who moved to Buffalo Flat a little less than ten years ago," Salado said. "We'd need some luck, but—"

"Luck might be on our side for a change," Millie finished for him.

He nodded. "It might be worth giving it a try. I'm willing if you are."

"Lord, Salado, you don't know how much I've been wantin' to get out of this town—"

A fist banged heavily on the door, and a man's voice called harshly, "Millie, you all right in there? We all heard you holler."

The voice belonged to Seth Brundage, who owned the saloon and got a large cut of all of Millie's earnings. He was a big, burly fella who served as his own bouncer and handled his own ruckuses.

Millie lifted her voice and called back, "Yeah, Seth, I'm fine. Just a misunderstanding. Everything's all right now." She motioned toward the corpse on the bed and shook her head. Salado understood what she meant. She didn't want to say anything about the old man dying on top of her. He was willing to go along with that, even though it meant he would probably have to dispose of the body later on. It shouldn't be too much of a problem. There were plenty of dark alleys in this town. The old-timer could be dumped in any of them. Since he hadn't been shot or stabbed or anything, when his body was found his death wouldn't look like foul play. Folks would figure he just stumbled into the alley and fell over dead. It wasn't that far from the truth.

Brundage didn't go away, though, like Salado thought

14

he would. Instead he asked through the door, "Is that damn tinhorn in there with you?"

There didn't seem to be any point in denying it. Everybody in the poker game had seen him come running up here. Salado moved closer to the door and called through it, not bothering to hide the irritation he felt.

"That remark is uncalled for, Seth," he stated.

The doorknob rattled, and something about the sound made Salado worry suddenly that he hadn't turned the key in the lock. It was too late now. Sure enough, the door was flung open a second later, and Brundage's big form bulked in the doorway, with several other men crowding close behind him, coming up on their toes to peer over his shoulders, expectant looks on their faces as if they hoped to catch a glimpse of Millie in the altogether.

"Uncalled for?" Brundage repeated. "I'll tell you what's uncalled for, Kyle." He held up a card, an ace of clubs, and Salado had a sinking feeling. "This extra ace that dropped out of your sleeve without you noticing when you jumped up, that's what's uncalled for, you damned cheatin' four-flusher!"

Salado tried to fight off the panic that started jumping around inside him. He said, "That card didn't come from my sleeve, Seth."

"The hell it didn't! Everybody at the table saw it!"

One of the other men looking over Brundage's shoulder pointed at the bed and asked in a worried voice, "Uh, is that old-timer *dead*?"

"What!" Brundage roared, apparently noticing the body on the bed for the first time. "What in blazes have you two done? Millie, did you kill that old man?"

"I never!" she exclaimed as she hastily adjusted her dress so that her left nipple didn't poke out above the neckline of it. "I mean . . . well, I guess . . . in a way . . ."

"She's a murderer!" howled one of the other men. "You heard her admit it! And that skinny card sharp is a cheat!"

15

This situation was quickly going from bad to worse, Salado thought. He had to nip it in the bud. Unfortunately, there was nothing he could do about his own problem, since that extra ace had indeed been up his sleeve. But he couldn't allow Millie to get in trouble for something that wasn't her fault.

"Millie didn't murder anybody," he insisted. "The old man just died. Look at him! You won't find a mark on him. His heart must have given out."

Seth Brundage came a step closer to the bed, a dark frown on his square face. "Well, I don't see any blood or anything," he admitted as he studied the corpse. "But this is still mighty fishy. And you're still a cheater, Kyle. Something's gotta be done about that—"

Millie stepped behind him, bent suddenly, scooped up the chamber pot just under the edge of the bed, and brought it crashing down on Brundage's head as she straightened. As it happened, the heavy pot was empty at the moment, but it still shattered with stunning force and knocked Brundage forward. He slumped onto the bed, sprawling across the old-timer's body.

"Salado, get out of here!" Millie shouted.

She had acted to save him from a beating or worse, Salado realized. He couldn't abandon her. There was a little matter of that possible fortune in hidden loot in Buffalo Flat, too. Millie was the only one who knew exactly what the old man had said before his years and his passion caught up to him. Salado grabbed her arm with his left hand while his right palmed the .38 from under his coat.

"Back off, gents," he advised as he menaced the men in the doorway with the pistol. "I'll ventilate the first man who reaches for a gun."

As always, there was one in the crowd who had to ignore that cautionary declaration. Salado saw the flicker of lamplight on cold steel and fired instinctively. The man who had drawn his gun, one of the poker players from

16

downstairs, yelped loudly as Salado's bullet plowed a furrow along his arm. His revolver thudded to the floor of the balcony.

There was nothing like a gunshot to make folks scatter. With a chorus of angry curses the men spread out, looking for cover. Smokepoles roared and slugs punched through the thin walls as Salado wheeled toward the room's lone window, dragging Millie with him. He went through headfirst in a shower of glass, and she came out right behind him. If Salado had thought for a second that the men after them might listen to reason, he would have stayed in the room and tried to talk their way out of this trouble. Now that the shooting had started, though, the men's fighting blood was up and they likely wouldn't stop pulling trigger until their guns were empty. It sounded like a small-scale Gettysburg in that room.

There was a narrow balcony outside the window that ran along the front of the saloon. Salado had known that when he went diving through the glass. He had several scratches that stung like blazes and hoped that Millie hadn't been badly cut by the glass.

"Grab some horses!" he told her as he fired a couple of shots back into the room, aiming high. So far he hadn't killed anybody in Kansas, and he would just as soon keep it that way. He glanced around in time to see Millie swing over the balcony's railing, hang by her hands, and then drop to the street below. With bullets whipping around his head, he couldn't take the time to be that careful. He ran at the railing, put a hand on it, and vaulted over.

An involuntary yell came from his mouth as he plummeted through the night. He landed hard and rolled over, feeling a twinge in his ankle. He hoped he hadn't broken it the way John Wilkes Booth did when he jumped from old Abe's box to the stage of Ford's Theater. As he scrambled upright, he saw Millie sitting astride a horse she had snatched from the hitch rail in front of the saloon. With her

17

skirt pulled up that way, her bare thighs gleamed enticingly in the moonlight.

Ah, well, no time for that now, Salado told himself as he grabbed the reins of the second horse that she held out to him. He got a foot in the stirrup and swung up, then banged his heels against the animal's flanks.

Up on the balcony, Seth Brundage shouted, "Hold your fire! You might hit the horses!"

Side by side, Salado and Millie galloped along the main street of the little cowtown. They had added horse stealing to their crimes of cheating at cards and fornicating with an old man until his heart gave out, Salado thought. Well, Millie was the one who'd done the fornicating, he amended mentally, and he was the card cheat. It was important to be clear about these things.

It was more important, though, to get the hell out of Kansas before the inevitable pursuit caught up with them.

Because with any luck, a fortune might be waiting for them in Texas.

Chapter 3

As he stood in the darkened doorway, Longarm rolled the unlit cheroot from one corner of his mouth to the other and wished that he could light it. The flare of a lucifer being scratched into life might give him away, though. Billy Vail had made it clear that this was a job requiring discretion. What he hadn't said was that it was going to be boring as hell.

"All we're doing is keeping an eye on this galoot," Vail had said that afternoon. "We want to know what he's doing, but we don't want him arrested."

"Must be a mighty special fella," Longarm had commented as he cocked his right ankle on his left knee and leaned back in the red leather chair in front of Vail's desk. It was all right to smoke in Vail's office, so Longarm snapped a lucifer to life with a thumbnail and held the flame to the tip of the cheroot clenched between his teeth. "What'd you say his name is?"

"Gammon. Jasper Gammon."

Longarm blew out a cloud of smoke and shook his head. "Never heard of him."

"That's probably because he's been in prison down at Canon City for the past nine years."

"Owlhoot, eh?"

"Banks, trains, stagecoaches," Vail said. "You name it, Gammon held it up at one time or another. He finally got caught when he stopped a stagecoach and one of the passengers blew his right arm off with a sawed-off shotgun. Gammon was lucky he didn't bleed to death right there in the road where he fell."

"So when he recovered he stood trial for the attempted holdup?" asked Longarm.

Vail nodded. "That was the only charge they could prove on him, but it was enough to get him eight years. He got another year tacked on to his sentence when he tried to escape after a couple of years inside."

"A one-armed man tried to bust out of the state pen?" Longarm frowned. "Must've been pretty desperate."

"Some men get a little crazy behind bars. You know that, Custis."

Longarm nodded. With his own restless nature, he figured he would go plumb loco if he was ever faced with having to spend years locked up in a cell. That was one more reason he was glad he was on the right side of the law.

"Gammon settled down after that," Vail went on. "Did his time and got released a few months ago. Since then, we've been keeping an eye on him."

Longarm blew a perfect smoke ring toward the banjo clock on the wall of Vail's office and said, "The fella's only got one arm, Billy. It don't seem likely to be that he'll go back to his desperado ways. Anyway, we usually leave folks alone until *after* they've committed a crime."

Vail sighed and ran a hand over his pink, balding scalp. "Normally, that's right. But a couple of years before he was arrested for that stage holdup, there was a rumor that Gammon was connected to the Cottonwood Station train robbery."

Longarm sat up straighter in the red leather chair. The holdup at Cottonwood Station had happened not long before he'd gone to work as a Deputy United States Marshal, but he'd heard of it, sure enough. Most lawmen west of the Mississippi had, and likely a good number of them east of the Father of Waters had, too.

"They never found all that money from the holdup, did they?"

Vail shook his head. "Not one single greenback. Somebody, somewhere, still has it."

"And you reckon Gammon knows where it is," Longarm said, seeing the light.

Vail shrugged. "That's what we're hoping. He's the only possible member of the gang that we know of. We don't really think he hid it. If he had the money, why was he still pulling penny-ante stagecoach jobs a year later?"

Longarm thought back over the facts of the case as best he could remember them. "That cash was on its way here to Denver to be taken out of circulation and destroyed, right?"

The chief marshal nodded. "That's right. We figure the gang got wind of the shipment somehow, maybe a tip from somebody who worked for either the railroad or the mint."

Longarm chewed on his cheroot as he thought for a moment. Then he said, "Did the government have a list of the serial numbers from those bills?"

"No. As soon as the money was stolen, law enforcement officers and banks all over the West were notified to watch out for an unusual amount of old bills."

"Maybe Gammon and his partners knew that would happen and figured it would be best to sit on the loot for a while," Longarm suggested. "They had the money, but they couldn't spend much of it right away without taking too big a risk of being caught. Maybe that's why Gammon was still holding up stagecoaches. He had to. Either that, or find honest work."

Vail laced his pudgy fingers together on the desk in front of him. "That theory has certainly been considered. It

21

makes sense. But now enough time has passed so that if Gammon knows where the money is—"

"He's likely to go after it," concluded Longarm.

"That's right. *That's* why we've been watching him. Your turn at the chore just hasn't come around yet." Vail paused. "Until now."

Longarm's jaw tightened and his teeth bit down harder on the cheroot. "Now, Billy," he said, "you know I ain't much of one for sitting around—"

"It's only fair," Vail broke in. "Other deputies have been keeping an eye on Gammon. You can take a turn at it, too, starting tonight."

Vail's brisk tone made it clear that he wouldn't tolerate any argument. He might look positively cherubic with his pudgy frame and pink scalp, but Longarm knew that before signing on with Uncle Sam's Justice Department, his boss had been a ring-tailed roarer of a Texas Ranger. With a sigh of resignation, Longarm nodded.

"Where do I find him?"

"He's been staying in a rooming house." Vail slid a piece of paper across the desk. "There's the address. He found himself an honest job, too, working at a wagon yard down the street."

"Don't seem like the sort of job a one-armed man would have," muttered Longarm as he committed the address of Gammon's rooming house to memory.

"No, but the reports we've gotten say that he works hard at it. From everything we can see, Gammon's walking the straight and narrow these days."

"But you don't believe it for a second, do you?"

Vail frowned. "The Treasury Department wants that money back. Gammon's our only potential lead to it."

"So we keep on watching him for how long? Ten years? Twenty?"

"Maybe it won't come to that."

Longarm sure as hell hoped it wouldn't. And if it did, he sure as hell didn't want the job.

But he had it, at least for tonight. Another deputy would relieve him in the morning and follow Gammon to the wagon yard, Longarm supposed.

The rooming house was on one of Denver's side streets. Diagonally across the way was a hardware store, which was closed for the night. Longarm had taken up his post in the darkened alcove of the store's entrance in time to see Gammon trudge home through the gathering dusk. A pair of field glasses had allowed Longarm to look in through the house's front window. He had watched Gammon eat supper with the other boarders, and then the one-armed man had climbed the stairs to the second floor, where his room was located. Longarm had seen the reports from the deputies who'd had this assignment earlier. He knew which window went with Gammon's room, so he wasn't surprised when the yellow glow of lamplight shone there a few moments later. He saw Gammon's shadow moving around against the curtains.

As he continued watching the house, Longarm turned the facts of the case over in his mind. He had gotten the file on the Cottonwood Station robbery from Henry, the spectacle-wearing young fella who played the typewriter in Vail's outer office. Over supper, before he took up his post, Longarm had gone through the file. Three men had held up that train. It seemed to Longarm that another likely scenario had Gammon being double-crossed by one or both of his partners. That would explain why he had still been living a life of crime a year after the big robbery. He had never gotten his share of the loot. Of course, the theory he had laid out for Billy Vail about the outlaws sitting on the money until things calmed down could be true, too. There was just no way of knowing yet.

Either way, though, he supposed that Gammon would

bear watching. If the man took off suddenly, or did anything else suspicious, chances were it would be tied in with those missing greenbacks.

Longarm's senses were still alert, but his mind drifted to pleasant thoughts of a certain young lady whose acquaintance he had made recently. She was a schoolteacher, and her contract had a morals clause in it. So she had to be careful about her behavior, or at least, about who found out what she was doing. If any of those ol' bluenoses on the school board ever saw her naked as a jaybird, on her hands and knees with her trim little rump stuck up in the air while Longarm took her from behind, rode her hard, and put her up wet, just the way she liked . . . Well, if that ever happened she likely wouldn't be teaching the little tykes much longer. That would be a real shame, too, because Longarm had talked to her enough to know that she really liked her job and was good at it. She just happened to enjoy screwing like a mink, too.

He sighed and chewed on the cheroot. As nice as those musings were, he needed to get his attention back on the job at hand. The lamp had just gone out in Gammon's room. The old outlaw had probably turned in for the night. That meant Longarm faced hours of standing there in the dark, trying to stay awake and alert, even though there was no real reason . . .

Something moved at the side of the house.

Longarm straightened from his casual stance. The movement didn't have to mean anything, but it was his job to check it out. His eyes narrowed as a couple of shapes entered the narrow alley between the house and a line of shrubs planted to form a border with the neighboring property. After a few seconds, Longarm's keen vision picked out the form of a man leading a saddled horse.

He lifted the field glasses. Using them at night presented some problems in getting oriented. Magnified darkness was still just darkness. But Longarm was an old hand at this sort

24

of thing, and it didn't take him long to get the glasses focused on the shadowy area beside the house. He saw another man step forward to meet the one with the horse. This second man took the reins. Awkwardly, he swung up into the saddle.

Did that awkwardness come from having only one arm? Longarm thought there was a good chance it did.

The mounted man leaned down from the horse and handed something to the man on the ground. Then he heeled the animal into motion and rode toward the rear of the house. The first man turned and walked back to the street.

By the time he got there, Longarm was waiting for him. With his right hand on the butt of the Colt holstered in a cross-draw rig on his left hip, the big lawman said, "Hold it, mister."

The man stopped short and put his hands up without being told to. "Oh, my God!" he exclaimed. "Is this a holdup?"

"Take it easy, old son," Longarm said, somewhat disgusted that he had been taken for a robber. He supposed he couldn't blame the fella for the mistake, what with it being dark and all. He went on, "I'm a U.S. deputy marshal."

"Oh." The man visibly relaxed. "Can I put my arms down?"

"I didn't tell you to hoist 'em in the first place. Who was that you met back yonder?"

The man lowered his arms and sounded confused as he asked, "You mean old Jasper?"

"Jasper Gammon? Fella with just one arm?"

"That's him. I work with him at the wagon yard. He asked me to saddle that horse and bring it down here to him after it got dark."

"Whose horse was it?"

"I'm not a horse thief," the man said, alarm coming back into his voice. "Jasper bought that horse fair and

25

square from our boss, Mr. Hudspeth. But he said he didn't have any place to keep it, so he left it at the wagon yard until tonight."

"Did he say where he was going?" Longarm asked sharply.

The man shook his head. "Nope. I know he's not coming back, though. Mr. Hudspeth paid him what he had coming this afternoon. Less the price of the horse, of course."

Longarm muttered a curse. Gammon was taking off for the tall and uncut, or so it seemed, anyway. Deputies had been watching him for weeks, and all he had done was go back and forth to work. Then tonight, on Longarm's first shift, he had to go and try sneaking out of town.

There was no time to waste. "You can go on about your business, mister," he said. "No need to say anything about this to anybody, I reckon."

"Whatever you say, Marshal. I don't want any trouble." The man hesitated. "I didn't do anything wrong, did I?"

"Nope. You can rest easy on that score."

The man sighed in relief as Longarm took off down the street, his long legs carrying him swiftly toward the livery stable he always used when he was in Denver. He wouldn't have a chance to check in with Billy Vail, but he would send a wire back to the chief marshal as soon as he could to let him know what was going on. Vail was sharp as a tack; he would figure it out pretty quick-like when both Longarm and Jasper Gammon turned up missing the next morning.

Ten minutes later, after rousting out the liveryman, Longarm rode back to the boarding house on a rangy buckskin gelding. He lit a match and studied the ground in the light from the flame. It wasn't difficult to pick up the tracks of the horse Gammon was riding. Unfortunately, when the trail reached another side street, the hoofprints disappeared into the welter of tracks that were already there.

Longarm reined in and sat there for a moment, studying on the problem. Gammon had turned south; Longarm was sure of that much. But had he continued in that direction? Heading that way would be a calculated risk.

Longarm didn't see what else he could do. He sent the buckskin south at a fast trot.

Chapter 4

By morning, Longarm was well south of Denver. He stopped in the settlement of Castle Rock, reining to a halt in front of a general store where a couple of old-timers sat in rocking chairs, shooting the breeze in the coolness of early morning.

"Howdy, gents," Longarm said to them with a friendly nod. "I'm looking for a pard of mine, was wondering if you'd seen him ride by."

"If it was in the last hour or so, we prob'ly did," replied one of the oldsters. "What's this fella look like?"

"Well, he's a mite longer in the tooth than me," Longarm said, recalling the description he'd read of Jasper Gammon in the file. "Got a red beard that's starting to go gray. And he's only got one arm."

The second old man snorted. "Why didn't you say that first? Yeah, a one-armed hombre rode by about thirty minutes ago. Stopped down the street at Maude's Café to get him some breakfast, I reckon."

Deliberately casual, Longarm nodded. "Much obliged. Maude's, you said?"

"Yeah, but the fella ain't there no more. He rode off on

the south trail, maybe five minutes ago. You can prob'ly catch him, if you hurry."

"Thanks," Longarm said. He wheeled his horse and sent the buckskin trotting along the street.

A feeling of relief filled him. His gamble had paid off. Jasper Gammon was only five minutes or so in front of him.

Of course, at this point he didn't want to catch the old rapscallion. He wanted to follow Gammon to wherever he was bound, because that was probably where the stolen loot was.

From a rise in the trail south of Castle Rock, Longarm looked out across the landscape spread before him and spotted movement up ahead. He drew the field glasses from his saddlebags and brought them to his eyes. The image seemed to spring at him as he focused in on the distant rider. He recognized the battered old hat and the sheepskin jacket Gammon had been wearing the night before when he came back to the rooming house from the wagon yard. There was no mistaking the pinned-up sleeve where Gammon's right arm was missing almost to the shoulder. When the trail curved around a boulder, Longarm got a look at the rider's profile as well and saw the jutting, reddish-gray beard.

Smiling in grim satisfaction, Longarm put away the field glasses and rode on, hanging back so that he wouldn't get too close to Gammon and maybe spook the old desperado.

Hunger began to gnaw at the lawman's belly not long after that. Longarm had left Denver in a hurry, without any chance to stock up on provisions. Now that he had Gammon in his sights, so to speak, he started to think about the details of what might prove to be a long chase. Early that afternoon, when Gammon stopped in a small settlement and went into the town's lone saloon to cut the dust, Longarm halted down the street at a mercantile and went inside to buy food. The whole time he was there, he kept an eye on Gammon's horse, which stood tied at the hitch rail in front of the saloon.

"Mister, you nervous about somethin'?" the storekeeper asked after a few minutes, as he filled Longarm's order.

"Nope."

"The way you keep lookin' outside, I thought maybe trouble was huntin' you." The proprietor frowned. "I don't want no shootouts in my store."

"Don't worry," Longarm assured him. "I'm plumb peaceable."

He bought flour, sugar, salt, beans, a side of bacon, and some jerky he could chew to tide him over until he made camp that night. Gammon finally came out of the saloon just as Longarm was settling up with the storekeeper. The man scrawled a receipt for the total. Henry would want that when Longarm turned in his expense vouchers for this job. The little fella was a bulldog when it came to seeing that everything was properly documented.

Gammon rode on south. Longarm let him get a slight lead, then set out after him. He wondered where they were going. New Mexico Territory lay to the south, but if Gammon curved west his route might take him all the way to Arizona. Likewise, a swing east would bring them to Texas. Hell, thought Longarm, if they rode far enough south, they'd be in Mexico.

It was a big land, with plenty of hiding places. Longarm resigned himself to the fact that he might be on Gammon's trail for a long time.

But if those stolen greenbacks were waiting at the end of the trail, the ride would be worth it.

A week later, saddle-weary and tired of eating his own cooking, Longarm rode through the West Texas cattle country. Mountains loomed purplish-gray in the distance to the south and west. To the east stretched the high range of the Edwards Plateau, running for more than a hundred miles until it dropped down into the hill country. This was prime range land, and although the spreads hereabouts weren't as big as the vast ranches up in the Panhandle, a man could still ride all day in places without crossing any boundary lines.

Gammon's trail had taken Longarm down through Raton Pass, across the corner of New Mexico Territory, and into the Texas Panhandle. From there Gammon had cut due south again. The deeper into Texas they had gone, the warmer the weather had gotten. Longarm still wore the brown tweed trousers from his suit and the white shirt, but he had long since packed away the coat and vest and string tie, and the sleeves of the shirt were rolled up over his tanned, muscular forearms. At the moment the garment was damp with sweat.

Gammon wasn't wearing his sheepskin jacket anymore, either. Instead of a shirt he had on the upper half of a pair of long underwear, originally red but faded now by time and washing to a pale pink. Suspenders attached to his denim trousers crossed over his shoulders. Longarm had studied him through the field glasses, taking care that a stray beam of sunlight didn't reflect off the lenses, and he could tell that the long ride had taken a toll on Gammon. The man's face was gaunt and haggard in the firelight each night when he made camp. But determination kept him going.

Hundreds of thousands of dollars in stolen money would give a man a powerful incentive to keep moving, thought Longarm.

A short time earlier today, at an isolated crossroads, a sign with an arrow pointing south had read BUFFALO FLAT. Longarm supposed that was the name of a settlement, probably a little cowtown that served as a supply point and maybe a shipping center for the ranches in the area. He wasn't sure if a railroad spur ran through these parts or not. Gammon might stop there, or he might not. The old outlaw had spent his nights on the trail, making camp rather than stopping in a town and renting a hotel room. Chances were, he didn't have much dinero and was trying to make it last as long as he could. He had visited a few saloons along the way, though, as thirst evidently trumped frugality.

The sun was dipping toward the western horizon. Longarm looked out across a long flat stretch bounded on the far side by a ridge. The flat was about a quarter of a mile wide, and Jasper Gammon had just reached the other side of it and started up the trail that led to the top of the ridge.

The flat crack of a rifle ripped through the warm, peaceful late afternoon, followed immediately by another shot that came so fast Longarm knew two men had to be doing the shooting. He reined in and leaned forward in the saddle, eyes narrowing as he peered across the flat. In the distance, Gammon jerked his mount around, spurred the horse down the ridge, and started back across the flat at a dead gallop. More shots popped and snapped.

Longarm heeled the buckskin into a run and started out onto the flat. It was obvious that somebody was shooting at Gammon. Longarm had no idea who it could be, but until he learned what had brought Gammon here to Texas, he wanted to keep the old owlhoot alive.

As the buckskin's hooves drummed along the trail, Longarm's jaw tightened. He wished he had taken the time and trouble to buy a rifle somewhere along the way. He had his Colt and plenty of ammunition, but that wasn't going to do him any good in a long-range fight.

Suddenly Jasper Gammon sagged in the saddle, and only a desperate grab at the saddle horn kept him from tumbling off the running horse. Longarm knew that Gammon had been hit. He could only hope that the wound wasn't too bad.

Dust rose into the sky along the ridge and caught Longarm's attention. The shooting had stopped, but only because the bushwhackers were chasing Gammon on horseback now. Longarm saw two riders careening down the trail. Smoke plumed from gun barrels and the sound of more shots drifted to Longarm's ears over the thunder of the buckskin's hooves. The would-be killers had opened fire again, but they would have to be phenomenally lucky to hit anything from the saddle of a galloping horse.

Gammon was still riding hard, but he was hunched over in the saddle now as if fighting against the pain of his wound. His horse ran aimlessly, with the bushwhackers closing in from behind and Longarm racing toward him from the front. More powdersmoke spurted from the gunmen. Longarm heard the whine of a bullet passing somewhere reasonably close to him. The riflemen had spotted him, he thought, and at least one of them was trying to keep him from reaching Gammon. That was pretty good shooting, considering the circumstances. He would have drawn his Colt and returned the fire, but he knew it would be a waste of lead and powder.

They were still taking some potshots at Gammon, too. One of them must have gotten lucky, because Gammon's horse suddenly stumbled as if hit. The horse tried to keep running, but its legs folded up underneath it. A cloud of dust billowed into the air as the horse went down and rolled over a couple of times. Longarm couldn't see Gammon anymore. If the horse had rolled over him, he was done for.

Longarm didn't slow his pace. He was still determined to reach Gammon before the bushwhackers did. If they got there first, they would finish off the old man, assuming he wasn't already dead. Longarm was close enough now he decided to risk some shots. He drew the Colt and squeezed off a couple of rounds, aiming high so that the bullets would carry as far as possible.

He was within a hundred yards of the spot where Gammon's horse had gone down. The bushwhackers were at least twice as far away. Longarm knew he would get there first.

But the odds were still two to one, and if the riflemen wanted Gammon dead badly enough, they would try to ride Longarm down and kill him, too.

The wind had carried some of the dust away. Longarm spotted Gammon lying on the ground a dozen feet away from the fallen horse, which lay on its side and didn't move. Longarm realized Gammon was still alive when the old desperado began trying to crawl behind the trunk of a fallen tree near the road.

Switching his attention to the horse, Longarm saw the butt of a rifle sticking up from a saddle sheath. That was a stroke of luck. He veered his own mount in that direction and leaped to the ground while the buckskin was still moving. Snagging the rifle from the saddle boot as he ran past the dead horse, he flung himself down next to Gammon, taking cover behind the log.

Gammon stared at him with eyes that were confused and bleary with pain. "I'm on your side, old-timer!" Longarm told him. "Let's give those bushwhackers a little hell!"

The wounded man managed to grin. A dark bloodstain stood out sharply against the pale pink of the long underwear he wore as a shirt. His hand shook a little as he drew his revolver and threw a shot over the top of the log.

Longarm hoped the old Henry rifle in his hands was fully loaded. He rested the barrel on the log, took aim, and fired. The Henry blasted and kicked hard against his shoulder. He worked the lever as fast as he could, jacking another round into the chamber. In a matter of five seconds, Longarm sprayed four shots at the charging bushwhackers.

One of the would-be assassins somersaulted backward out of the saddle, driven off his horse by a solid hit from one of Longarm's slugs. The other man glanced at his fallen partner and reined in. He was too far away for Longarm to make out any of details about him except the black, broad-brimmed Mexican sombrero he wore. It made a good target. The big hat leaped into the air as Longarm put a bullet through its tall crown.

That did it. The surviving bushwhacker had had enough. He jerked his horse around and put the spurs to it.

Longarm threw another couple of shots after the man as he raced off toward the ridge, but neither of them found their mark. The gunman kept moving and never slowed down until he had topped the ridge and gone out of sight. Longarm didn't know if he slowed down even then.

Gammon let out a groan and slumped down beside Longarm. Turning toward the old-timer, Longarm saw that the bloodstain had spread even more. Gammon was hit bad.

Longarm threw a glance at the sprawled body of the man he had shot. The man hadn't moved since bouncing once when he hit the ground, and Longarm was fairly sure he was dead. A fella in his line of work got to where he could tell about things like that. Still, you could never be sure, and more than one star-packer had been shot down by an owlhoot he had thought was defunct. Longarm squeezed Gammon's shoulder with his left hand and said, "Hang on. I'll be right back."

He stood up and ran over to the fallen man, keeping the rifle trained on him the whole way. The bushwhacker had landed on his back, with one leg twisted underneath him at a funny angle. He wasn't feeling the pain of the busted limb, though. His wide-open eyes stared sightlessly at the brassy Texas sky.

Longarm turned and hurried back to the log where he had left Gammon. Gammon lay on his back, too, but his chest still rose and fell in an irregular rhythm. His breath rasped harshly in his throat. Longarm heard a little whistling sound every time Gammon took a breath and knew that the bullet had punched through one of the man's lungs.

Gammon wouldn't last much longer. There was no time for subterfuge. Longarm leaned close to him and said ur-

36

gently, "Gammon! Gammon, listen to me! Where's the money? What happened to the money you took off the train at Cottonwood Station?"

Gammon blinked a couple of times. His mouth opened and closed, but no sound came out.

"I know you were in on the holdup at Cottonwood Station." Longarm had to get through to him and get an answer, otherwise this long trip down here to Texas was all for nothing. "Gammon, tell me where the money is!"

Gammon's hand came up suddenly and clawed at Longarm's sleeve with surprising strength. The man's eyes opened wide. His mouth worked. Bright red blood dribbled from the corner of it.

"Blaze!" he gasped. "Buffalo Flat! Blaze . . ."

What the hell did that mean? Longarm wondered wildly. A fire in Buffalo Flat? Could the money be there? Gammon *had* been heading in that direction.

Gammon's head fell back, and Longarm thought he was a goner. But not all the life had slipped out of the old outlaw's body just yet, and he breathed one more word. Longarm leaned closer, trying to make it out.

"Har . . . ker . . ."

Then, with a ghastly rattle in his throat, Jasper Gammon died.

Hunkered on his heels next to the corpse, Longarm frowned in thought. *Harker.* He was sure that was what Gammon had said. Somebody's name, more than likely. It almost had to be. Then Longarm put it together with what Gammon had said before. "Blaze Harker," Longarm said softly. It *was* a name, and he recognized it from somewhere. But for the life of him, he couldn't recall where he had heard it before.

Looking down at Gammon's lifeless, bearded features, Longarm shook his head. From the way the old outlaw had slipped out of Denver on the sly and headed straight for Texas, Longarm knew that he'd had a definite destination in mind. Maybe it was Buffalo Flat. Maybe somebody named Blaze Harker lived there and could give him the answers he needed. There was only one way to find out.

But wherever he had been going, whatever he had been after, Jasper Gammon's journey was over now. It had ended where everyone else's did, sooner or later, across the Great Divide.

Chapter 5

Longarm caught his own horse first, then rounded up the horse that had been ridden by the dead bushwhacker. Now that there was more time, he took a better look at the man's corpse. The bushwhacker was roughly dressed in range clothes, with the coarse, beard-stubbled features of a hard-case. Longarm considered a couple of theories. The bushwhacker and his sombrero-wearing partner could have jumped Gammon intending to rob him. Gammon didn't look like a very lucrative victim, though. The other theory was that somebody had posted the two ambushers out here with orders to kill Gammon when he came riding along.

Had Gammon been lured into a trap? Longarm frowned as he turned over that thought in his mind. It certainly seemed possible.

Since Gammon's horse was dead, Longarm had to put both bodies on the bushwhacker's horse. The animal was skittish about carrying one corpse, let alone two, and it took a while before Longarm had both bodies tied down on the back of the horse. The sun had set while he was working at it. A rosy orange glow remained in the western sky, however, and provided enough light for him to follow the trail up the ridge and through an area of rougher, wooded terrain before he came to another long, flat stretch. This one had a cluster of lights in the middle of it. Longarm figured he had found the settlement of Buffalo Flat.

Darkness had settled down all the way by the time Longarm reached the town. As he suspected, it was a typical West Texas cowtown, with a main street that ran for several blocks lined by frame buildings that housed the community's business. The side streets, where folks lived, had a mixture of frame and adobe structures. A white-washed church with a tall steeple sat at the far end of the settlement, and a large building near it was probably the school. On the northern edge of town, two livery barns faced each other across the street. As he rode along, leading the other horse with its grisly burden, Longarm saw a couple of emporiums, a barbershop, a blacksmith shop, a hardware store, a saddle maker, an apothecary, two doctor's offices, a fairly nice restaurant, a hotel, a bank, a couple of hash houses, and eight saloons.

Plus a marshal's office with a little stone jail behind it. That was where Longarm headed with the two bodies.

The windows of the marshal's office were lit by the yellow glow of a lamp. Longarm tied the horses to the hitch rail in front of the place, stepped up onto the porch, and went in without knocking.

The man sitting at the desk in the little office had been dozing. He came awake with a confused sputter and finally focused his gaze on Longarm. "Evenin', mister," he said in a high-pitched voice. "What can I do for you?"

Longarm wasn't overly impressed by the local badge-toter. The man was middle-aged, with curly brown hair and a considerable paunch. The tin star pinned to his vest looked like it hadn't been polished for a while. Longarm said, "Are you the marshal?"

"That I am. Hannibal Gibbs is the name. Is there a problem?"

40

Longarm jerked his thumb over his shoulder. "I've got a couple of dead men out there," he said bluntly.

Gibbs's eyes widened in surprise, losing some of their sleepiness. "Dead men?" he piped. "What in tarnation happened? Did you kill 'em?"

"One of them," admitted Longarm. "But he was doing his damnedest to kill me at the time, so I reckon it all evens out."

Gibbs stood up. "Yeah, I reckon. What's your name, mister?"

Longarm didn't hesitate. "Parker," he said, which wasn't strictly a lie since that was indeed his middle name, given to him by his ma back in West-by-God Virginia. "Custis Parker."

When he had first stepped into the marshal's office, Longarm had been undecided whether or not he would reveal his true identity to the local lawman. That would have been the proper thing to do, of course, since he was a federal officer operating in this man's jurisdiction. But one look at the slovenly marshal had told Longarm that Gibbs couldn't be trusted, at least not yet, and so he'd used one of his customary aliases instead. The leather folder containing his badge and bona fides would remain safely in his pocket for the time being, until he had gotten the lay of the land in Buffalo Flat.

Hannibal Gibbs rubbed his stubbly chin. "Well, Parker, I reckon you'd better tell me what happened. Where'd this killin' take place?"

"A couple of miles north of here."

"My authority ends at the town limits, but if I'm gonna take charge o' them carcasses, I want to know what I'm lettin' myself in for." Gibbs gestured toward a black, pot-bellied stove in the corner. "Might still be some coffee in the pot. Pour yourself a cup and spin your yarn."

Longarm frowned. "Shouldn't you send for the undertaker first?"

41

"Those fellas ain't gonna get any more dead than they already are," said Gibbs with a shake of his head.

Longarm shrugged and nodded. "All right, then." He got a cup of Arbuckle's and then launched into a somewhat edited account of the afternoon's events, leaving out any mention of him being a federal lawman and trailing Jasper Gammon to Texas. In the story Longarm told, he was just drifting along when he came upon a lone man being ambushed and pursued by two killers. Naturally, he said, he had pitched in to help.

"But by the time I downed one of the skunks and chased the other one off, the fella they were after had been hit." Longarm inclined his head toward the street. "His body is out there, along with the hombre I ventilated."

"The fella was dead by the time you got to him, huh?"

Longarm couldn't tell if Gibbs's apparently casual question concealed a deeper interest. But since he was here to find out if there was any connection between Gammon and somebody in Buffalo Flat, Longarm knew he would have to stir things up to get any answers. That meant poking at things folks didn't want poked at.

"No, he lived for a few minutes, long enough to tell me his name."

"What is it?"

"Jasper Gammon."

Gibbs shook his head. "Never heard of him. Must've been a drifter. He say anything else?"

"Just another name . . . Blaze Harker."

That made Gibbs's eyes narrow. "Blaze Harker," he repeated.

"Name mean something to you?" asked Longarm, apparently idly.

Gibbs pulled open a drawer in his desk and began pawing through it. "I ain't quite sure," he said. "It's familiar, though."

Longarm knew what the local lawman meant. Harker's

42

name tickled some memory in the back of Longarm's head, too, but so far he hadn't been able to dredge it up.

"Here ya go," Gibbs said a couple of minutes later. He pulled a paper out of the drawer and slapped it down on top of the desk. "Take a look," he invited.

Longarm leaned forward. The paper was a wanted poster, and it had Blaze Harker's name printed on it in big letters. There was no drawing, just a description, and underneath it more printing explained that Harker was wanted in four states and two territories for various crimes including bank robbery, train holdups, and murder.

That was more than enough to bring back the memory for which Longarm had been searching. Blaze Harker's name had been bandied about quite a bit in law enforcement circles, back in the days when Longarm had first started toting a badge. But he had never been caught, as far as Longarm knew, and he had either died or retired from his life of crime, because he hadn't been heard of in years. That was why the memory of his name had faded. Longarm checked the date on the reward dodger that Gibbs had dug out of his desk and saw that it was more than ten years old.

"This fella who got shot," Gibbs said a little breathlessly, "you reckon he could've really been Blaze Harker, instead of Jasper Gammon?"

Longarm considered the possibility, but only for a second before discarding it. Gammon had been known as an outlaw in his own right, a decade earlier. Longarm wondered suddenly, though, if Blaze Harker could have been one of the other two desperadoes who had pulled off the Cottonwood Station robbery.

In his pose as a drifter himself, he wasn't supposed to know about such things. So he put a finger on the description of Harker printed on the wanted poster and said, "This doesn't sound like him. According to this, Harker was tall, over six feet, and clean-shaven with black hair that had a

43

white streak in it. Reckon that's how he got the name Blaze. The fella I tried to help out was shorter than that, with red hair and a beard. And only one arm."

Gibbs heaved a sigh of disappointment. "One arm, eh? Well, I reckon he couldn't be Harker, then. I thought for a minute you might have a reward comin' to you, Parker. The offer's still good, more'n likely."

What Gibbs had thought was that if Gammon and Harker turned out to be the same person, he would find a way to get his own hands on some of that reward money, if not all of it. But Longarm didn't say that. Instead he said, "I don't know anything about Harker, or about this fella Gammon, either, except that he got bushwhacked. I just want to turn the bodies over to somebody in authority and be done with it."

"Yeah, yeah, I understand." Gibbs reached for a shapeless brown hat that sat on the cluttered desk. "Come on, let's have a look at the carcasses."

They went outside to find that several people were standing near the hitch rail, looking curiously at the corpses without coming too close to them. One of the citizens of Buffalo Flat called, "What's going on, Marshal? Those men are *dead*!"

"Yep, they sure enough are," Gibbs agreed amiably as he stepped over to the horse carrying the two bodies. He caught hold of the bushwhacker's head by the hair and lifted it casually so that he could study the dead man's face in the light that came through the open door of the office. After a moment he lowered the man's head and said, "Nope, never seen him before."

"The other one's Gammon," Longarm said quickly. He wasn't sure why, but he didn't want Gibbs jerking the old outlaw's head up like that. It was undignified somehow.

Gibbs spoke to one of the bystanders. "Go fetch Doc Maxwell." To Longarm he added, "Doc's the coroner, as well as one of our local sawbones."

"I reckon there'll have to be an inquest," Longarm said.

Gibbs sighed. "Yeah, we got to do things all proper-like. Buffalo Flat's a civilized place, you know. If you're tellin' the story straight, though, there shouldn't be any problem."

"It happened just like I told you, Marshal," Longarm said, which was true as far as it went. He had just omitted any mention of his real identity and the case that had brought him to Texas on Gammon's trail.

A few minutes later, Doc Maxwell, who was a small, mostly bald man with a sour expression on his face, came up and said, "These the men who are dead?"

"Well, I sure hope so, Doc," Gibbs replied.

"I've sent for Wally Pettingill, told him to bring his wagon and haul the bodies over to my office. I'll have a look at them, then let Wally have them."

Longarm guessed that Wally Pettingill was the local undertaker. Gibbs talked to the doctor for a minute, then turned to Longarm and said, "You'll be around town for a day or two, Parker?"

"Sure. I'm in no hurry to leave."

"Not headed any place in partic'lar, eh? And don't care when you get there, neither."

Longarm nodded. "That's about the size of it, Marshal." Let Gibbs think he was just a drifting cowpoke. "How's the hotel in this town?"

"Well, there're no bedbugs, leastways none that I've heard of. And it's never more'n half full, so you won't have any trouble gettin' a room."

"Much obliged for the advice." Longarm untied the buckskin's reins from the hitch rail. "Which livery stable is the best?"

"Both about the same, just take your pick."

Longarm led the buckskin back up the street and stabled him. He left his saddle with the hostler but took the saddle bags and carried the Henry rifle he had taken off Jasper Gammon's horse. He didn't have any extra ammunition for the Henry, but he figured he could pick some up at one of the general stores in the morning.

As he approached the hotel, the front door of the establishment opened and a man and a woman stepped out onto the porch. They moved to one side, out of the way, as Longarm climbed the stairs to the porch. He glanced at them, not really paying much attention to them. Both of them were young, the woman around nineteen or twenty, the man a few years older. He was lighting a cigar as he and his wife or ladyfriend paused on the porch. He wore a brown suit and a cream-colored Stetson.

Feeling eyes on him, Longarm looked at the woman again. Like the man, she was well-dressed, in a bottle-green traveling outfit that was several shades darker than her green eyes. She was fair-skinned, with red hair pulled into a demure bun at the back of her head. She smiled at Longarm, and he touched a finger to the brim of his hat and nodded politely to her as he passed. "Ma'am," he said.

"Good evening, sir," she replied, her voice pleasant.

Then Longarm went on into the hotel and forgot all about the man and woman on the porch.

Chapter 6

"I know I've never really complained about your profession," Salado said in a low voice as his teeth clenched on the cigar in his mouth, "but do you have to be such a whore *all* the time?"

Millie looked over at him, frowning in confusion. "What the hell are you talking about?" she asked quietly.

He jerked his head toward the front door of the hotel. "That fella who just went inside."

Millie stared at him, unable to comprehend why he was upset. "All I did was say good evening to him."

"When a woman like you says good evening . . ." Salado shook his head. "Well, it packs a considerable punch, let me tell you."

For a moment, Millie couldn't speak. When she could, she said coldly, "You're insane. Should I never speak to another man again, just so you won't think I'm being a whore?"

Salado took the cigar from his mouth and tapped the ash over the porch railing into the street. "Never mind," he said. "I reckon I made too much out of nothing."

Millie gave a little ladylike snort. "I'll say you did."

"Let's get our minds back on what brought us here," suggested the gambler. "Money."

They had arrived in Buffalo Flat that afternoon, driving a buggy that they had bought in one of the settlements to the east. The ride down from Kansas had been a swift, arduous one. At first they had moved as fast as possible on horseback because they didn't want any pursuit catching up to them. Salado had done some shrewd horse-trading to keep them in fresh mounts. He had also sat in on a few poker games to get them traveling money. His natural skill with the pasteboards had been enough to make them flush. He hadn't even needed to cheat. At each stop, they bought supplies and then moved on hurriedly, riding down through Indian Territory until they splashed across the Red River and into Texas. Salado figured they were safe then; nobody, not even a sorehead like Seth Brundage, would chase them that far over what had happened in Kansas.

Millie wasn't so sure. From what she had seen of Brundage, he was the sort of gent who held a grudge like a bear hug, never letting go of it until it was dead. She had urged Salado not to drag his feet as they moved on. Besides, the sooner they got to Buffalo Flat, the sooner they could find that fortune in stolen greenbacks. Assuming, of course, that the money was hidden somewhere in the vicinity of the settlement . . .

In Fort Worth, Salado had run their cash into a good-sized stake. They headed south and west, through Granbury, Stephenville, and Brownwood, then turned almost due west from there, headed toward Buffalo Flat. They wanted to seem very respectable, Salado had said, so they bought the buggy, dressed well, and drove into the little cowtown like a couple of swells. When they checked into the hotel as husband and wife, Salado had dropped hints that he was a wealthy businessman looking for investments. Nothing attracted money like more money, Salado had told Millie once they were up in their room.

They hadn't figured out yet exactly how they were going to proceed, but Millie knew Salado would think of something. He was smart in most ways, even though he was sometimes dense about women. She didn't have any interest in that tall fella who had just gone into the hotel. Although he *was* a handsome cuss, with that tanned, hard-planed face and spreading longhorn mustaches. Under other circumstances . . .

She put those thoughts out of her head. She and Salado were here to get rich, not for any other reason.

"What do we do first?" Millie asked.

Salado puffed on the cigar for a moment and then said, "Tomorrow morning we'll pay a visit to the local banker and establish ourselves. We can't rush things. I'm as anxious to get my hands on that loot as you are, but we'll have to take it slow and easy, work our way into the trust of the community."

Millie didn't say anything. She wasn't sure Salado had the right idea, but she couldn't think of anything else to do. Slow and easy it would have to be, at least for now.

When Longarm came down to the hotel dining room for breakfast the next morning, he felt folks watching him and saw a couple of the waitresses whispering to each other behind their hands as they glanced toward him. That was enough to tell him that word had gotten around town about the two dead bodies he had brought into Buffalo Flat the night before.

One of the waitresses, in black dress and white apron, came over to the table where he sat down. She was a plump, pretty gal, but she seemed nervous as she said, "Good morning, sir. Would you like coffee?"

Longarm nodded as he dropped his hat on the floor next to his chair. He wanted to tell her that she didn't have to worry, he wasn't going to haul out his hogleg and shoot her, but instead he just said mildly, "Yes, ma'am, I sure would. You might as well bring a whole pot."

"And for breakfast?"

"Steak if you've got it, ham or bacon if you don't, couple or three fried eggs, a pile o' hash browns, tall stack o' flapjacks, and maybe some biscuits and honey."

"Oh," the waitress said. "All right."

"I know it's what you'd call a hearty breakfast," Longarm said with a grin. "I'd try to tell you that I'm still a growin' boy, but I don't reckon you'd believe me."

The waitress laughed, not quite so nervously now. "You just wait right there, sir, and I'll be back with your coffee."

Let folks gossip, Longarm thought as he sat there and unobtrusive swept his gaze around the room. He was here to stir things up, so that was a good start.

The waitress returned with a pot of coffee and cup and saucer. As she poured the steaming black brew, she said, "The cook says he'll have your breakfast out here in a jiffy, Mr. Parker."

"You know my name, do you?" asked Longarm.

She glanced around and lowered her voice to a more conspiratorial tone as she answered, "I reckon just about everybody in Buffalo Flat has heard of you, Mr. Parker. It ain't every day that somebody brings in a couple of bodies, if you don't mind me speaking plain."

"I don't mind at all," Longarm assured her. "What's your name?"

"Paula," she said. "Paula Danville."

"What are folks saying about me, Paula?" he asked as he lifted his coffee cup.

That made her nervous again. "Oh, I don't know that I ought to be repeating gossip . . ."

"It's all right."

"Well . . ." She looked around again. "Folks say you must be some sort of gunfighter." She looked at him expectantly, as if she were waiting for him to confirm or deny the rumor.

Longarm just smiled serenely. He was saved from having to answer by the arrival of Marshal Hannibal Gibbs, who spotted Longarm and came bustling over to the table.

"Mornin', Paula," he said in his squeaky voice to the young woman. "How's about bringin' me a cup, so I can share Mr. Parker's coffee?"

"I don't recall inviting you to join me, Marshal," Longarm said coolly.

Gibbs waved a pudgy, blunt-fingered hand. "I figured you'd want to be sociable, seein' as how we'll be goin' over to the inquest in a while."

Longarm shrugged and nodded. "You're welcome, I suppose. Bring that other cup, Paula."

She bustled off. Gibbs looked after her and sighed. "That's a mighty pretty filly. I like a gal with some meat on her bones. If I wasn't as old as I am—"

Longarm changed the subject by saying, "You find out anything else about those two hombres I brought in?"

"You mean the fella you killed and the one who got bushwhacked?" said Gibbs in a loud voice. He shook his head. "Nope. Neither of 'em had anything that would identify them in their pockets. That bushwhacker, though, was carryin' damn near a hundred dollars."

That told Longarm something. A hardcase like that probably wouldn't have so much money on him unless he had gotten it recently and hadn't had a chance to spend it yet. The most reasonable explanation was that somebody had paid him and his partner a hundred dollars each to kill Jasper Gammon. The presence of the money seemed to rule out a random robbery attempt.

"The inquest shouldn't amount to much," Gibbs went on. "The way you told me the story, it's pretty cut-and-dried."

"That's the way it happened," Longarm said.

"I ain't doubtin' you. I don't reckon the coroner's jury will, either. Shouldn't take more'n a few minutes, and then you'll be free to go, Parker."

Longarm sipped his coffee. "Actually, I was thinking

51

about staying around for a while. This strikes me as a pretty nice little town."

"Oh, it is, it is."

"Lots of good cattle spreads hereabouts?"

Gibbs nodded. "There's a few. Lookin' for a ridin' job, are you?"

"I've been known to do some cowboyin'," Longarm said.

Gibbs regarded him shrewdly. "Just what else do you do?" he asked, and now his voice, while still neutral, had lost its amiable, jolly tone.

"Whatever I run across that needs done," Longarm answered flatly.

"That so? Some folks are sayin' you're a gunman, but I don't have any paper on you, Parker. I know, 'cause I looked through all my reward dodgers, and they go back a good number of years."

"I'm not wanted, Marshal," Longarm said honestly. He tried to steer the conversation back where he wanted it to go. "The ranchers around here, they've all been in the area for a while? Ten years or more?"

"Well, some of 'em have been here that long. Not all of 'em, though." Gibbs rubbed his jaw in thought. "Thad Calhoun moved in and started his spread about five years ago, I'd say. Mitch Ferrell's had the Circle F eight or nine years. They're the newest. All the other ranchers in the county have been here fifteen or twenty years, I reckon. It was about twenty years ago that this area settled down enough for the cowmen to come in. A few tried before that, but the Comanches always got their stock . . . and their hair."

Longarm nodded. Nothing Gibbs had said surprised him. He knew quite well that the Texas frontier hadn't spread this far until not long before the Civil War. And there hadn't been much expansion during the Late Unpleasantness itself because so many men had been back east, fighting in the Confederate Army. Since then, however, with the expansion of the beef market and the arrival of the railhead in Kansas, ranching in Texas had boomed. The days of the great northern cattle drives were over now that rail lines had extended into the Lone Star State itself. Ranchers could drive their herds the relatively short distance to Fort Worth instead of all the way to Abilene or Dodge City. The cattle business was still strong.

A fella could set up a mighty nice spread with only a part of the loot that had been stolen at Cottonwood Station, Longarm told himself, thinking of the cattleman named Mitch Ferrell that Gibbs had mentioned. Ferrell had arrived in the vicinity of Buffalo Flat at just about the right time. But if he had been involved in the Cottonwood Station robbery, how could he have used much of the money? Every bank in the whole Southwest would have been watching for a bunch of old bills to show up.

Of course, that didn't mean that bank tellers would be diligent about it. Longarm had noticed a bank down the street as he rode into Buffalo Flat the night before. He would have to have a talk with the bank manager and see if he had been notified to keep an eye out for the bills.

Gibbs went on, "I don't know if any of the spreads around here are hirin' right now. Spring round-up's over. There'll probably be some herds movin' up the trail to Fort Worth, though, so you could ask around."

Longarm nodded. "I'm obliged for the information, Marshal." He looked toward the door leading into the kitchen and saw Paula emerging with a big platter in her hands. "There's my breakfast."

"Don't let me stop you from eatin'," said Gibbs.

Longarm tried not to sigh. It looked like he was going to have company for this meal whether he wanted it or not.

A few minutes later, while he was eating, the couple he had seen on the porch of the hotel the night before came into the dining room. Longarm would have smiled and nodded to the pretty redheaded woman as she went by, but she

53

kept her head turned as if she were deliberately trying not to notice him. That was a mite puzzling, he told himself. He couldn't think of anything he might have done the night before to offend her. Hell, he had barely spoken to her.

But if that was the way she wanted to be, it was fine. After all, she didn't have anything to do with the real reason he was here in Buffalo Flat.

"There, I didn't even look at him," Millie said quietly as she and Salado sat down at a table across the room from the tall stranger.

"I told you I was sorry," he hissed. "I won't say anything more about it. Let's think about what we're doing, instead."

Over breakfast, they conversed in low tones about their plans for the day. Salado had worked out the story they would tell the banker, and he wanted to go over the details one last time before they approached the man.

Millie tried to pay attention, but from time to time she felt her eyes straying to the mustachioed stranger. He was sitting at a table with a fat man who wore a tin star pinned to his vest. Given her experience with her uncle, along with things that had happened since then, she didn't like or trust lawmen. She wondered if the stranger could be one. If he was, that would be a damned shame.

She was skillful enough at making a man think he was the center of her world so that Salado never noticed she wasn't paying attention to him part of the time. Millie noticed that the young woman who waited on their table talked quite a bit to the waitress who attended to the stranger. Maybe they were gossiping about the tall man whose face was tanned to the color of old saddle leather, she thought. When Salado excused himself for a few minutes to visit the privy out back, Millie called the mousy girl over and asked quietly, "Do you know who that gentleman is, the one over there sitting with the sheriff?"

"He's not the sheriff, he's Marshal Gibbs," the waitress

answered in the slightly surly tone that most unattractive females used in dealing with the much prettier Millie. "And the fella with him, the one you asked about, is some sort of gunslinger. I hear he brought in two dead men last night, and he killed them both because he didn't like the way they looked at him!"

Millie doubted that. The tall man might be a gunfighter; he wore a well-used Colt in a cross-draw rig on his left hip and from what she had seen of him when he entered the hotel the night before, he moved with catlike grace despite his size. He didn't have the eyes of a ruthless, cold-blooded killer, though. He might shoot a man, but he would have to have a good reason for it, she decided.

"Do you know his name?" she murmured.

"It's Parker. Custis Parker, I think."

Millie had never heard of him. Working in saloons, she had heard a lot of gossip and idle talk about men who were fast on the draw. If Custis Parker was famous for his gun-handling, it was under a different name. Which was entirely possible, of course.

Parker and the marshal got up and left the dining room. A few minutes later, Salado returned. "Are you finished?" he asked.

Millie drank the last of her coffee and nodded. "I'm ready," she said.

"Let's go, then," he said as he put down a bill to cover the cost of their meal. He held her chair, then settled his hat on his head and took her arm. Together, they strolled out of the hotel and headed down the street toward the First State Bank of Buffalo Flat.

Millie glanced around, hoping she might see Custis Parker. But there was no sign of the tall, handsome stranger, and she had no idea where he had gone.

Chapter 7

Buffalo Flat had a town hall, an airy frame building where the old-timers gathered to play dominoes whenever it wasn't being used for official business. Several bearded, elderly men were among the spectators as the inquest got underway, in fact, impatiently waiting for it to be over so they could get back to the bones.

The old-timers weren't the only ones there, however. There were quite a few spectators, drawn by the novelty of what had happened. They wanted to hear the facts of the case for themselves. Doctor Maxwell, the local coroner, sat at a table in the front of the room and gaveled the proceedings to order. Quickly, he empanelled a jury of six from the townsmen gathered in the audience. The jurors took their seats proudly in hard-bottomed, straight-backed chairs.

"All right," Maxwell said crisply. "Let's get to it." He looked at Longarm. "Mr. Parker, get up here and tell your story."

Longarm was sworn in and testified, sticking to the story he had given Marshal Gibbs the night before. It wasn't strictly the truth, the whole truth, and nothing but the truth, but he figured it was close enough for government work.

When Longarm was finished, Maxwell asked, "Do you

know the identities of either of the men whose bodies you brought into town last night, Mr. Parker?"

"I know the one-armed man said his name was Jasper Gammon," replied Longarm. "But do I know for a fact that he was telling the truth? No, sir, I don't. As for the other fella . . ." Longarm shook his head. "I never saw him before. All I can say for sure is that he and his pard ambushed that old-timer."

"All right, you can step down and take your seat."

Longarm left the witness chair and returned to his place next to Gibbs. He was a little surprised a moment later when the coroner called Gibbs to the stand. Longarm didn't know what the marshal could add, other than confirming that Longarm hadn't changed his story since the night before.

"Marshal, do you know anything about either of the two dead men?" asked Maxwell.

"Well, I asked around town about that so-called bushwhacker," Gibbs began.

There was nothing "so-called" about it, thought Longarm. The dead man *was* a bushwhacker. Had been one, anyway, until Longarm fatally ventilated him.

"Nobody knew his name," Gibbs went on, "but a few gents in the saloons seemed to remember an hombre who looked like him bein' around for the past week or so. And he had a pard who wore one o' them big Mexican hats, like Mr. Parker said the other bushwhacker had on. They kept to themselves, though, just drank a little and then moved on. I reckon it's safe to say they was both drifters. Wouldn't surprise me if they were wanted, but I didn't come across no paper on 'em."

"What about the other man, this Jasper Gammon?" asked Maxwell.

"Well, now, that's a different story," Gibbs said, and Longarm sat up a little straighter. He could think of only one thing that Gibbs might have discovered about Gammon.

58

The marshal went on, "While I was lookin' through my old wanted posters, I found this one." He took a folded piece of paper from his pocket and handed it to the coroner, who unfolded it and smoothed it out on the table in front of him. Gibbs continued, "You can see for yourself, Doc, that's a reward dodger for an outlaw named Jasper Gammon. The name's the same, and except for him not havin' just one arm, the description fits, too."

Maxwell frowned. "Yes, yes, it does." He looked at Longarm. "Consider yourself still under oath, Mr. Parker. Do you know anything about this?"

Longarm spread his hands. "Not a thing, Doctor," he lied.

Flat-out lying under oath rubbed him the wrong way. It wasn't quite the same thing as leaving out a few facts. But he wasn't ready just yet to spill the whole story, so he didn't have much choice.

Maxwell went on, "This wanted poster is from more than ten years ago. The man could have lost an arm in that time. Have you gotten in touch with any other law enforcement agencies in an attempt to find out more about Jasper Gammon, Marshal?"

Gibbs nodded. "I sent wires to Ranger headquarters in Austin and also the U.S. Marshals' office in Denver. Ain't heard back from either one of 'em yet."

Longarm's mouth tightened under the sweeping mustaches. Gibbs might look lazy and unkempt, but the local lawman had stolen a march on him. Longarm had intended to send a wire to Billy Vail today, bringing him up to date on what was going on. Now it was even more imperative that Longarm get in touch with his boss so that Vail would know he was working undercover here in Buffalo Flat.

"Well, for the moment I think we can assume that the one-armed man was Jasper Gammon," Maxwell was saying. "That doesn't tell us why those two drifters wanted him dead, but for the purposes of this inquest, it doesn't matter. We're simply trying to determine how those two men met their death and if there was any crime committed." He looked at the row of jurors. "Would the jury like to retire for deliberations?"

The six men talked quietly among themselves for a moment, and then one of them, a burly, bearded man who wore a blacksmith's apron, stood up and said, "Ain't no need for that, Doc. We got a verdict."

Maxwell nodded gravely. "Let's hear it, then."

"We rule that the fella who said he was Jasper Gammon was bushwhacked and murdered by that other fella, who was legally gunned down in self-defense by Mr. Parker there."

"Good enough for me," said Maxwell as he brought the gavel down on the table. "The verdict of the coroner's jury will be so entered. This inquest is concluded." He looked at Longarm. "Mr. Parker, consider yourself free to go."

Longarm nodded. "Thanks, Doctor. But I reckon I might stay around Buffalo Flat for a spell."

Maxwell arched his eyebrows in surprise. He advised, "Try not to kill anyone else while you're here."

"Yes, sir," said Longarm. "Only if they don't give me any choice."

The key to being rich, Salado had figured out, was acting like you were rich. If you did that well enough and for long enough, then the reality would just naturally follow. So far in his life it hadn't quite worked out that way, but he still believed in the idea. So he let a little arrogance creep into his voice as he told the bank teller that they wanted to speak to the manager.

The teller, a slick-haired gent with buck teeth, nodded and said, "Yes, sir, I'll go ask Mr. Stroud if he can see you. What's the name?"

"Kyle," Salado replied. "J. Robert Kyle."

The teller nodded again and left the window to go

through a door off to the side of the bank. Millie leaned closer to Salado and whispered, "Is that your real name?"

"Joseph Robert Kyle," he said.

She smiled. "I'll bet you were called Joe Bob when you were a kid."

His breath hissed between gritted teeth. Even though she was teasing, her shot had hit the mark. He had indeed been called Joe Bob, and he had hated it. That was a farm boy's name, what you called a gangling kid in patched overalls, with bare feet and a dirty face and no prospects other than a life of hard work and an early grave. That was exactly who he had been and the sort of life he had faced, until he discovered that he was skilled at cards and almost as adept with a six-gun. From that moment on he had known he was destined for better things.

The teller came back before Salado had to say anything else. The man waved a hand toward the door and said, "Go right in, sir."

Salado and Millie entered the bank manager's office to find a man in his thirties standing behind a desk with his hand outstretched. As Salado shook with him, the man said, "Mr. Kyle? Pleased to meet you. I'm Charles Stroud."

"You're the manager of this bank?" asked Salado.

Stroud grinned. "Manager and owner," he said. He was a handsome man, with thick dark hair, rather bushy side burns, and a sharply-planed face.

Salado raised an eyebrow. "Pardon my surprise," he said. "You seem to be a rather young man to own a bank."

"I inherited it from my father." Stroud nodded toward a framed photograph on the wall, which showed a distinguished-looking man with a bald head and an impressive mustache and goatee. "The late Benjamin Stroud. He founded the Bank of Buffalo Flat, rest his soul." The banker turned his smile on Millie. "And this is Mrs. Kyle, I assume."

"That's right," Salado said. Since they were sharing a

room at the hotel, they had to pretend to be married. He wished they had bought Millie a cheap wedding band, but he hadn't thought of it on their way here, and he couldn't very well try to buy one in Buffalo Flat. "My wife Mildred."

Stroud took her hand and smiled some more. "It's a great honor and pleasure to make your acquaintance, Mrs. Kyle." He waved expansively. "Please, sit down, both of you, and tell me how I can help you."

When they were seated, Salado said, "I find myself in the position of needing to make some business invest-ments, Mr. Stroud, so I've been traveling around Texas looking for something suitable. As the local banker, I thought you might be the best person to advise me."

"I see. Of course, I'll be glad to be of assistance in any way I can. Cigar?" Stroud took the lid off a humidor and pushed it across the desk.

"Don't mind if I do," Salado said as he reached forward to pluck one of the tightly-rolled cylinders of tobacco from the humidor. He sniffed it approvingly and tucked it into his coat pocket to smoke it later.

Stroud leaned back in his chair and steepled his fingers. He asked, "What led you in particular to Buffalo Flat?"

"The place has a reputation as a nice, stable community, just the sort of town in which the local business establish-ments thrive."

Stroud nodded. "Yes, we're a small town, but it's a good place to live and do business. Were you looking to establish an enterprise or invest in an existing one?"

"I prefer to invest in an existing one. One that has been in business for, oh, nine or ten years at least. Stability is paramount to me, Mr. Stroud."

"The world would be a better place if everyone were as cautious and prudent as you seem to be, Mr. Kyle. Let me tell you about some of our local commercial establish-ments. There's no guarantee, of course, that any of the owners would be interested in taking on an investor."

"Of course," Salado murmured.

For the next few minutes, Charles Stroud discussed the businesses in Buffalo Flat. Salado paid close attention, making mental notes of all the businesses that had been started about the same time as the Cottonwood Station holdup. By asking apparently innocent questions, he was able to eliminate some of them as possibilities, such as the businesses that had been started by people who had lived in Buffalo Flat for years beforehand. Someone who had spent his whole life in this little cowtown was unlikely to have been up there in eastern Colorado robbing a train, although it wasn't impossible, of course. Salado concentrated more on men who had moved to the area at the right time.

When Stroud had finished with his rundown of the businesses in Buffalo Flat, Salado said, "What about the ranches in the area?"

"Oh, I don't think you'll find that any of the local cattlemen are interested in taking on a partner," Stroud said with a shake of his head. "Most of them are old-timers. They were the first settlers in the area, you know, before the town was even here."

"Surely some of them aren't so set in their ways . . ." Salado prodded.

Stroud frowned in thought. "Mitch Ferrell and Thad Calhoun have been here the shortest amount of time, I suppose. One of the first loans my father made was to Mitch when he bought the Circle F. Thad came to the area a few years after that. I could speak to them if you'd like, but I really think you might be better off concentrating your efforts here in town."

"Don't say anything to them yet," Salado said. "You've given me a great deal of information, Mr. Stroud, and I think I need time to mull it over before I decide on the best course of action."

"Certainly." The banker turned his smile on Millie.

63

"Mrs. Kyle, you haven't said anything. What do you think of your husband's investment plans?"

"Oh, I leave all that sort of thing to Robert," Millie answered easily. "He's so much smarter about business than I am."

"You do yourself a disservice, ma'am. Surely a woman as lovely as yourself is also quite intelligent."

"Yes, she's very smart," Salado said, annoyed that Stroud would flirt with Millie like that right in front of him. Of course, back in Kansas he had seen men in Seth Brundage's saloon paw her all over before taking her upstairs to bed, and that hadn't bothered him then. Why was he becoming so unaccountably jealous these days? Regardless of the reason, he had to stop it. Having this hick banker enthralled by her might come in handy.

They stood up and shook hands all around again, and Stroud walked them to the door of the bank. "If there's anything I can do for you, don't hesitate to call on me," he told them, and his smile at Millie made it clear that the offer extended to her, as well.

As they walked away, arm in arm, Millie said quietly, "Aren't you going to complain because I was acting like a whore again?"

"On the contrary, darlin'," Salado forced himself to say. "Before this is all over, you may have to act a lot more like a whore than that."

Chapter 8

When Longarm and Marshal Gibbs stepped out of the town hall following the inquest, the marshal asked, "What are you plannin' to do now, Parker?"

Longarm slipped a cheroot from his pocket and put it in his mouth unlit. "Reckon I'll take a day or two to figure out my next move," he replied. "I'll probably ride out to some of the ranches and find out if they're hiring."

"All right. As long as you abide by the law, you're welcome here in town. Best be careful while you're ridin' around, though. That sombrero-wearin' bushwhacker is still on the loose. He might try to settle the score for his pard."

Longarm's eyes narrowed. Was that a subtle threat, or was Gibbs genuinely concerned about his safety? Longarm couldn't tell.

The two men parted company, Gibbs waddling off toward the marshal's office while Longarm walked up the street to the livery stable where he had left the buckskin. He checked on the horse and then headed for the telegraph office, which he had noted earlier was in the same building as the stagecoach station. There was no rail line in Buffalo Flat, but it was on the Fort Worth to El Paso stagecoach run, and according to a chalked schedule board hung up on the station wall, the coaches came through twice a week.

Longarm went inside, got a yellow telegraph flimsy and a stub of a pencil at the counter, and laboriously printed out a message to his Uncle Billy in Denver, pausing from time to time to lick the pencil lead as he apparently struggled to form the words. There were enough misspellings in the message so that the operator gave him a faint smirk of contempt when he read it.

"That'll be forty cents," the man said.

Longarm paid him and asked, "That'll go out right away, won't it?"

"Yes, I'll send it right now."

"Much obliged," said Longarm. He lingered just outside the open door of the office, ostensibly to light his cheroot. His keen ears picked up the clicking of the telegraph key as the operator sent the message just as Longarm had written it. He was a competent telegrapher himself when he needed to be and was able to follow the dots and dashes without much trouble.

Longarm blew out a cloud of smoke in satisfaction. Billy Vail would see right through the barely literate words to the hidden message underneath and would know that Longarm was on the trail of the missing money in Buffalo Flat. Longarm wasn't certain yet that the answer to the mystery was here, but his finely honed lawman's instincts told him that it was. Buffalo Flat would certainly do with some more investigating, at the very least.

But to do it properly, he might have to take at least one of the locals into his confidence. He pondered that as he walked slowly along the street, and by the time he had reached the First State Bank of Buffalo Flat, he had made up his mind. He opened the door and walked into the bank.

"I need to see the fella in charge," he said to the buck-toothed teller behind the wicket.

"Again? He's a popular man this morning," the teller

muttered, which made Longarm frown in confusion. But before the big lawman could ask what he meant by that, the teller said, "Just a moment, sir," and vanished through a nearby door.

He came back a minute later and none too politely told Longarm to go on in. Longarm stepped into the office and closed the door behind him. A gent with bushy sideburns sat behind a desk, the pen in his hand scratching as he wrote in a ledger. He barely glanced up at Longarm as he asked, "Yes, what is it?"

Longarm knew why the teller and now the bank manager were treating him sort of brusquely. They figured him for a drifting cowhand or, if they had heard the gossip, a notorious gunfighter. To get the sort of cooperation he needed, he was going to have to take a chance. He slipped the leather folder from his pocket, opened it, and placed it on the desk in front of the bank manager. The man glanced at it, then sat up sharply and looked again at the badge and bona fides. His startled gaze lifted to his visitor's face.

"You're—"

"Deputy U.S. Marshal Custis Long," said Longarm quietly. "And I'd appreciate it if you'd keep that to yourself, Mister . . . ?"

The bank manager came to his feet. "Stroud, Charles Stroud," he introduced himself. "This is my bank. What can I do for you, Marshal?"

Longarm put his identification away. "I'm here on a case, and I need some information. I've got to warn you, though, I'm working undercover and this has got to be kept quiet for now."

"You can count on my discretion, Marshal," Stroud assured him. "Please, have a seat. Cigar?"

"No thanks," Longarm said as he took a chair in front of the desk. He smiled as he added, "These three-for-a-nickel cheroots are a mite foul to some people, but they suit me."

"That's fine." Stroud sat down and clasped his hands together on the desk. "What do you need to know?"

"Have you ever heard of the Cottonwood Station holdup?"

Stroud frowned in thought. "I'm not sure. It sounds vaguely familiar, but I can't quite place it."

"About ten years ago, three men took over a little train station in Colorado and stopped and robbed a train on its way to Denver with a big shipment of old currency that was due to be taken out of circulation and destroyed."

Stroud nodded eagerly. "Of course. I remember reading about that. I wasn't in the banking business at the time, so it didn't really mean as much to me as it might have later."

"A notification was sent out so that bank tellers could watch out for the old money," Longarm continued.

Stroud nodded. "Yes, that would be standard procedure. I can tell you right now, though, Marshal, that no stolen money has ever passed through this bank, at least not in the time that I've been running it. We're very diligent about such matters."

"And how long has that been?" asked Longarm.

"Since I took over the bank? Let's see, it's going on seven years now. My late father Benjamin founded the bank." Stroud looked up at a portrait of a bald man with a goatee that hung on the wall. "He passed away suddenly."

"Sorry to hear it," Longarm murmured.

"I had been working for him for a couple of years as head teller, so I was able to take over the running of the bank. I can assure you that prior to that, my father was careful about such things as well. If any of that stolen money had shown up here, the authorities would have been notified immediately."

"You sort of jumped to the conclusion that I'm on the trail of that loot," Longarm said.

Stroud shrugged. "Why else would you be here? A U.S.

marshal shows up and talks about missing money. It's an easy assumption to make."

"Yeah, I reckon so," Longarm admitted.

"Has your investigation turned up a link between that train robbery and Buffalo Flat?" Stroud asked eagerly.

"We've got reason to believe one of the fellas responsible for the holdup might be here," Longarm replied. "I've just started looking around, though. Just got into town last night."

The banker's eyes widened. "You're the gunman everyone's been talking about! The man who brought in those bodies last night!"

Longarm leaned forward. "You're the only one who knows I'm really a lawman, Mr. Stroud. I ain't even told your local badge-toter. That's why I need you to keep it under your hat."

"Of course. You have my word on it. I've told you that none of the missing bills have come through the bank. What else can I do to help you?"

"Tell me about anybody who might have shown up here in Buffalo Flat about nine or ten years ago and started a business or a ranch or something like that."

The question provoked even more of a response than Longarm had expected. Stroud leaned back in his chair, looking astonished, and muttered, "Good Lord!"

"What is it?" asked Longarm sharply.

"Marshal, you're the second person this morning who has asked me such a question."

Longarm bit back a curse of surprise. "Who else was interested in that?"

"A young businessman named J. Robert Kyle. He and his wife Mildred came to see me just a short while ago. According to Mr. Kyle, he wants to make some investments in the area, but he's only interested in a stable situation, such as a ranch or a business that has been in operation for nine or ten years."

Longarm's brain worked rapidly. "You know this fella Kyle?" he asked. "Is he from around here?"

Stroud shook his head. "I'd never seen either him or his wife before they came in this morning. But I don't see how they could possibly have any connection to that train robbery or the missing money."

Neither did Longarm. "What did these folks look like?" he asked.

"Well, they're both young, but something about them makes them seem older than their years. He's around twenty-five, tall and slender with brown hair. Mrs. Kyle is a few years younger and a very attractive young woman, if I may be so bold as to say so. She's almost as tall as her husband and has red hair."

The couple he had seen on the hotel porch the night before and in the dining room this morning, thought Longarm. But as Stroud had said, how could they be tied in with the Cottonwood Station robbery? Both of them would have been just kids when the holdup took place.

"Perhaps this is just some sort of odd coincidence," Stroud went on. "It's certainly possible that someone looking for a good investment would visit the local bank and ask just such questions as Mr. Kyle did."

Longarm gave a skeptical grunt. "Yeah, maybe. But I reckon those two will do with some looking into."

"Please be discreet, Marshal. If Mr. Kyle is a potential customer for the bank, I'd hate to have him scared off."

"No offense, Mr. Stroud, but I reckon the job I'm here to do is a mite more important than some bank deposits."

"Of course, of course," Stroud said hurriedly. "I didn't mean to imply otherwise. As an officer of the law you have to pursue whatever leads you may find."

Longarm nodded. "Now, what about the fellas who moved into the area not long after that holdup at Cottonwood Station?"

Stroud smiled as he said, "I won't have any trouble an-

70

swering that question, since I just went over the information with the Kyles not that long ago." For the next few minutes he talked about the businesses in Buffalo Flat and the cattle spreads in the area. "Mitch Ferrell might be your best bet as far as the ranchers go," said Stroud. "He came here nine years ago, and he was in his late thirties then, I'd say. He's a tough man, too. Several years ago he caught three men venting the brands on some of his cattle. He and his cowboys hanged all three of the rustlers, right then and there. The county sheriff wasn't happy about it, but he didn't pursue charges against Mitch. There have been other instances, too, of fistfights and gunplay whenever someone crossed Ferrell, but at least in those cases no one was killed."

Longarm nodded slowly, thinking about what Stroud had told him. He was going to have to pay a visit to Mitch Ferrell's Circle F, he decided.

Stroud went on, "Now that I know what you're looking for, Marshal, I'd say that among the men here in town, you should concentrate on Barney Rosson, Ed Schmitt, and Jim Carver."

Longarm cast his brain back over the information Stroud had given him. "Rosson's the blacksmith, Schmitt owns one of the livery stables, and Carver's the saddlemaker?"

"That's right. All of them came to Buffalo Flat between nine and ten years ago, and all of them are old enough to have been part of the gang that held up that train." Stroud leaned forward as a thought occurred to him. "The shooting yesterday that resulted in those two dead men . . . does that have something to do with this case?"

Longarm had already put most of his cards on the table. It was a little late to start being cagey. "There's a good chance the man who was bushwhacked, Jasper Gammon, was one of the three outlaws who grabbed that money at Cottonwood Station. He's been in prison in Colorado for the past nine years and just got out not long ago. We'd been keeping an eye on him, thinking he might lead us to the money once he was released. He slipped out of Denver and lit a shuck for Texas. I was on his trail the whole way, until those two hombres jumped him and killed him."

"So you think . . . let me get this straight . . . you think one of the other men came to Buffalo Flat, brought the stolen money with him, and established himself here in a new identity."

Longarm nodded. "That's the theory I'm going on right now, based on some things Gammon said before he died."

Stroud held up his hands, palms out. "I don't want to know any more, Marshal. To tell you the truth, I sort of wish you hadn't told me as much as you did. If you're right, there's an outlaw and a murderer here in Buffalo Flat. It might even be somebody I know, like Mitch Ferrell."

"You don't have to worry," Longarm told the banker. "I just needed to find out for sure that none of the stolen money had come through here. If the fella I'm looking for really is around here, he's still sitting on that cache of loot."

"Ten years is a long time to wait," Stroud said.

"Yeah, but when we're talking about that much money, an hombre can afford to be patient."

"I suppose." Stroud sighed. "I hope I've been of some help to you, Marshal, but I have to admit, I don't like the idea of knowing that someone I've done business with is really a desperado."

"They come in all shapes and sizes," said Longarm as he stood up. "But you're out of it now, Mr. Stroud. I shouldn't have to bother you again."

"Well, if there *is* anything else I can do to help, don't hesitate to ask." Stroud got to his feet. "What are you going to do now, Marshal?"

"Just poke around some more and see what I can find out about Ferrell, Rosson, Schmitt, and Carver. Until I find out different, I'm going on the assumption that one of them is the gent I'm looking for." Longarm paused and then added, "I got to figure out how that young fella and his wife tie in to this, too, if they really do."

Stroud shook his head. "That one is beyond me, I'm afraid." He came around the desk. "Let me walk you out."

They left the office and went into the lobby of the bank. As they did so, a woman entered through the front door and came toward them, a smile on her face. That smile was for Stroud, Longarm realized, and he was a lucky man to be getting it. The woman was well-dressed in a dark blue dress and a matching hat that perched on an elaborate arrangement of thick blond curls. She was exquisitely shaped and had bright blue eyes that smoldered with a carefully banked intensity. Longarm could tell that even though she gave him only a brief glance as she came up to him and Stroud.

"Good morning, Charles," she said in a husky voice. "I hope I'm not interrupting anything."

"Not at all, my dear," said Stroud. "I was just finishing my conversation with . . ."

He hesitated, and Longarm realized that Stroud either hadn't heard or had forgotten the alias he was using. The banker was quick-witted enough, though, to realize that he couldn't introduce his companion as Deputy Marshal Custis Long.

Longarm took off his flat-crowned, snuff-brown Stetson and nodded politely to the woman. "Custis Parker, ma'am," he introduced himself, getting Stroud off the hook. "At your service."

She gave him a gloved hand. "I'm pleased to meet you, Mr. Parker."

"Mr. Parker is a potential depositor," Stroud said. "Mr. Parker, this is my fiancée, Miss Karen Wilkes."

"Ma'am," Longarm said again. "Mr. Stroud here is a lucky fella, if you don't mind my saying so."

Karen Wilkes laughed. "Of course not. In fact, I'm flat-

73

tered." She linked arms with Stroud. "But I think I'm the lucky one."

"Well, congratulations to the both of you." Longarm put his hat on, unwilling to spend any more time on pleasantries. With a nod, he said, "I'll be seeing you."

He left the bank and turned once again toward the livery stable. It was pure chance, but he had left the buckskin at the stable owned by Ed Schmitt, who had come to Buffalo Flat a little more than nine years earlier to open the business. Longarm wanted to take a ride out to the Circle F, but first he would have a talk with Schmitt and see if he could get any information out of the liveryman.

He stopped short when he saw someone else standing in the open double doors of the stable, talking to Schmitt. The pretty redhead was nowhere in sight, but the fella talking to Schmitt was none other than the man who called himself J. Robert Kyle.

Chapter 9

Salado had left Millie in Buffalo Flat's lone dress shop, explaining that he thought the liveryman would be more likely to speak plainly without a woman around. She didn't care for being dismissed that way, but she knew that once he had an idea in his head, it was almost impossible to change it.

That was how she came to be standing by the shop's front window, pretending to be admiring some bolts of cloth, when she saw the tall, handsome gunfighter named Parker walk past, headed up the street. She watched him, admiring the cat-like grace of his movements, and then frowned slightly as he suddenly stopped short and then stepped back between a couple of buildings so that she couldn't see him anymore. Millie craned her neck to look up the street, wondering what had provoked that reaction on Parker's part, but all she saw was Salado standing there talking to the middle-aged man who owned the livery stable.

Was it possible Parker didn't want to approach the livery stable because Salado was there? That didn't make sense. Why would Parker care?

Physical attraction and curiosity . . . it was a potent, maybe even dangerous, combination. She turned to the woman who ran the dress shop and said, "Excuse me, is there a back door out of here?"

"Of course, ma'am," the woman said, gesturing between a couple of dress dummies. "Why do you—"

The question came too late. Millie pushed past her, jerked the door open, and stepped out into the alley behind the building before the woman could finish.

Longarm stood there thinking. The presence of Kyle at the livery stable didn't have to mean anything. Kyle and his wife had to have arrived in Buffalo Flat somehow, and since there hadn't been a stage in several days, that meant the most likely way was by buggy. Kyle could have stabled his team at Schmitt's and parked the buggy out back.

It was hard for Longarm to believe that much in coincidence, though. He seemed to be dogging Kyle's trail this morning. The man had to have some connection with the stolen money, although Longarm was danged if he could figure out what it was.

"Hello."

The voice from behind him made him stiffen. Instinctively, his right hand started across his body toward the butt of the Colt on his left hip. But he was able to control the reaction, because he realized that the voice belonged to a woman. At the same time, he was angry with himself for letting anyone slip up on him like that.

He turned, and somehow he wasn't surprised to see the tall redhead standing there. She smiled at him and went on, "Why are you lurking back here?"

"Wasn't lurking, ma'am," Longarm replied. "I was just, ah . . ."

"It looked like lurking to me. You're that gunfighter, Mr. Parker, aren't you?"

"My name's Parker, but I don't lay claim to being a gunfighter," he said.

"My name is Millie Ames. Mildred Ames Kyle, I

mean." She blushed prettily. "I haven't been married all that long. Sometimes I forget to use my husband's name."

Politely, Longarm touched a finger to the brim of his hat. "Pleased to meet you, ma'am." He asked himself what the hell sort of game she was playing.

"I noticed you watching my husband, Mr. Parker," she said boldly. "I was wondering what your interest in him is."

Longarm put a frown on his face. "Ma'am? I'm afraid I don't know what you're talking about."

She nodded toward the livery stable and said, "That's him right over there, talking to the man who runs the stable. Are you an outlaw, Mr. Parker? Do you plan to rob my husband? I should tell you, he's not as helpless as he might look. He's pretty good with a gun."

Longarm's head was spinning. He said, "Mrs. Kyle, I don't have the foggiest notion what you're talking about. I'm not an outlaw, and I ain't planning to rob anybody, let alone your husband."

He started to turn away, but she stopped him by putting a hand on his arm. Leaning closer, she moistened her lips with her tongue and then said, "I didn't mean to insult you. I just . . . I guess I just wanted an excuse to talk to you. Ever since I saw you last night at the hotel, I . . . I've been thinking about you . . ."

Good Lord, thought Longarm. She was standing so close to him now, and even though she was tall for a woman she had to tip her head back a little to look up into his eyes, and he felt the heat coming off her like she was the sun on a Texas summer day. She moved her hand up his arm until she could reach behind his neck. Holding him there, she came up on her toes and pressed her lips to his.

Longarm was utterly baffled, but he had to admit that her mouth felt and tasted mighty fine as she kissed him. He didn't return the kiss, though, or take her into his arms. After a moment she pulled back suddenly, gave a dainty little gasp, and said, "I . . . I'm so sorry! I had no right—" She

77

broke off and turned sharply, obviously intent on running away.

Longarm's hand shot out and closed around her arm, stopping her in her tracks. "Hold on there a minute, ma'am," he said. "I think you forgot something."

As she turned her head toward him, he saw fires blazing in her green eyes. "Let go of me, you bastard!" she hissed. "I'm warning you—"

"I'll let go of you as soon as I get my wallet back," he said as he used his other hand to search her. His touch skimmed over the curves of her body under the dress and then his hand dipped into a pocket. It came back out with the old leather wallet she had slipped out of his pocket as she kissed him. "I've been back east a time or two," he went on. "They've got pickpockets in those big cities who make a living stealing folks' purses. No offense, ma'am, but I reckon you'd starve if you had to do that."

She began to curse him, and the venom that spilled from her lips was at odds with the appearance she was trying to project as the wife of a young businessman. She talked more like a soiled dove from some cattletown saloon.

Longarm let go of her and she backed away from him. He said, "I don't have any interest in you or your husband, Mrs. Kyle, so I reckon we ought to pretend that none of this ever happened."

That was a lie, of course. He was more intrigued than ever by the mysterious young couple and still wanted to know what connection, if any, they had with the case that had brought him here. But she didn't have to know that.

"I don't know how that wallet got in my pocket," she said. "And if you go to the law, I . . . I'll claim you tried to attack me! You pulled me back in this alley and molested me!"

"I'm not going to the law," Longarm told her. "Like I said, we'll just forget about this."

She had jerked around enough while he was holding her so that some of her hair had come loose, and the red strands now hung around her face and fell to her shoulders. Longarm thought her slightly disheveled condition made her more attractive than ever, but he wasn't worried about such things at the moment. He was much more interested in what role she and her husband played in all this.

She continued backing away until she finally turned and ran, ducking around a corner and disappearing. Longarm let her go. He was confident, however, that he was not done with Mildred Ames Kyle or her husband. He would be seeing both of them again.

He put his wallet away and turned back toward the main street. Even if she had gotten away with the wallet, she wouldn't have found much in it. A couple of dollars, a few innocuous papers, that was all. Most of his money was hidden in his boots, and the thin leather folder containing his badge and identification papers was in another pocket.

Maybe she was just a thief, he told himself. That was certainly possible. Her husband's story about being a well-to-do businessman looking for some investment opportunities could be nothing but a crock of lies. Or she could have been trying to find out who Longarm really was by stealing his wallet. But why would she suspect that he was anything other than what he appeared to be?

Several times during his long and tumultuous career, Longarm had found himself literally at sea, adrift in an ocean filled with dangers. Even though Buffalo Flat was hundreds of miles from the coast, he was beginning to feel like he had stepped into some pretty deep waters here, too . . .

"You did *what*?" Salado practically yelped when Millie told him what had happened in the alley. They were strolling arm-in-arm along the street toward the hotel.

"Hush!" Millie said. "I was just trying to help."

"Just trying to lure that gunfighter into your bed, that's what you were trying to do!" Salado kept his voice low, but he couldn't keep the emotion out of it.

"I wanted to find out who he is, and taking his wallet seemed to be the best way to do that. He wasn't supposed to realize what I'd done until after I was gone."

"So you distract him by acting like a whore and then steal his wallet." Salado shook his head in disbelief.

"I *am* a whore, remember? How many times do I have to remind you of that? How else am I supposed to think? That's all I've ever been!"

He stopped and rested his hands on the railing along the boardwalk. "All right," he said slowly. "The damage is done. Let's just calm down, and you can tell me what you found out."

"Well . . . nothing, really," Millie said miserably. "I never got to look in his wallet."

Salado nodded. "How do you know he has any connection with us?"

"I don't, not for sure. But I was watching him, and I saw the way he acted when he saw you talking to that liveryman. It was just too suspicious, Salado."

"Robert," he said emphatically. "You're supposed to call me Robert."

With a sigh, she nodded. "I know, I know. It's hard to break old habits."

"With you it certainly is."

The acid-tongued comment made her want to slap him. Instead she reined in her temper and said, "He claimed not to know what I was talking about, but he was lying. I'm sure of it." She gave voice to the thought that had been lurking in the back of her mind. "He knows about the money, Sala—I mean, Robert. Somehow he found out about it, and he's after it, too."

Salado shook his head. "That's impossible. He's just some drifting gunman. How could he know about it?"

"I'm just a soiled dove and you're just a gambler, and we know about it," she pointed out.

"Yes, but only because of what that old man told you before he died."

"Maybe Farley told the same thing to other people. Maybe he told that man Parker, if that's his real name, about the money, too."

Salado rubbed his jaw in thought. "I suppose it's possible," he said slowly. "We don't have any way of knowing who Farley talked to or what he said before he came into Brundage's saloon. But it's just so far-fetched . . ."

"Far-fetched things happen sometimes," she insisted. "That could be why he was on his way to the livery stable."

"Or maybe it was because his horse is stabled there," Salado said dryly.

Millie shook her head. "Trust me on this, Salado—I mean, Robert. My intuition tells me that man is trouble."

"All right, we'll keep an eye out for him," agreed Salado. "But in the meantime, we have to keep searching for a lead to the money."

"What did the stableman say?"

"The banker was right. Schmitt came to Buffalo Flat and started that livery stable about nine years ago. He admitted that right off while I was pretending to chat with him. But what Stroud didn't know was that Schmitt had been running another livery before that, down in New Braunfels, close to San Antonio."

"Are you sure about that? He could have been lying. If he came here to establish a new identity, wouldn't he have a phony story all made up and ready to go? That stolen money could be buried in the barn right now!"

"Schmitt told me all about his life in New Braunfels in long, boring detail, Millie," said Salado. "If he was lying, then he's wasting his time in Buffalo Flat. He ought to be back in New York or somewhere, acting in plays." The gambler shook his head. "No, I'm convinced Ed Schmitt isn't our man."

"Then what do we do now?"

"We've just started looking," he said. "We still have several other possibilities. We'll split up. I'll talk to the saddlemaker, and you take the blacksmith. Then we'll get the buggy and both take a ride out to see that rancher, Ferrell."

"Let's do it the other way around," she suggested. "I'll talk to the saddlemaker. Why would I have any business with a blacksmith?"

Salado shrugged. "All right. Just watch out for that fellow Parker. If we keep tripping over each other, I'll be forced to agree that you might be on to something about him. He could be a danger to us."

"And what do we do if he is?"

Salado looked at her coolly. "Dangers have to be removed . . . whatever it takes."

Chapter 10

By the time Longarm had spent ten minutes with the garrulous Ed Schmitt, he knew that the liveryman wasn't the person he was looking for. In fact, he would have been willing to bet that the man didn't have a larcenous bone in his body. Longarm certainly couldn't see him masterminding the Cottonwood Station robbery.

He did learn one thing of interest from his conversation with Schmitt, though. The liveryman said in his slight German accent, "Folks sure are friendly today for some reason. Just a little while ago, some young fella came by and talked to me for a while, wanted to know all about my life before I come to Buffalo Flat."

"Is that so?" asked Longarm, trying not to sound too interested.

"Yah. He said he was thinkin' about buyin' an interest in my business, but even after I told him I didn't want to take on no partners, he kept talkin'."

That confirmed what Longarm already suspected: J. Robert Kyle and his wife Mildred were on the trail of that stolen money, just like he was. He wondered if those were their real names, or if they were even married.

He still wanted to talk to Rosson and Carver, the blacksmith and the saddlemaker, but he thought it was likely the Kyles had already moved in on them. From what he had heard of Mitch Ferrell, the rancher seemed more likely to be the man he was looking for, so maybe if he rode on out to the Circle F he could get there before his young competitors did. He said to Schmitt, "I'll be taking that buckskin of mine out for a while."

"Yah, *gut*. Want me to saddle him for you?"

"No thanks."

Five minutes later, after getting directions from the stableman to Ferrell's ranch, Longarm rode out of Buffalo Flat and headed south.

It was a pretty spring day with a few puffy white clouds floating high in the arching blue sky. Big sky country, they called this, and they were right, although there were a lot of places west of the Mississippi that fit the description equally well.

As he rode along, Longarm turned over all the aspects of the case in his mind. Ever since Jasper Gammon had been released from the Colorado state prison at Canon City, he had been watched. If Kyle and Mildred—Millie, she had called herself first, he remembered—had visited Gammon, that fact would have been noted by the deputies who had kept an eye on him. But Gammon could have written to them without the watchers ever knowing about it. Maybe one of the young people was related to Gammon. Maybe he had asked them to meet him in Buffalo Flat.

But if that were the case, why hadn't the old outlaw told them Blaze Harker's new identity? Why did they seem to be just as much in the dark about who they were really looking for as Longarm was? Deep in thought, he frowned, tugged distractedly at his earlobe, and then ran his thumbnail along his jawline. Those nervous habits were a good indication just how puzzling this case really was.

Was it possible that Kyle and Millie were coming at this from an entirely different angle? They could have found out some other way that the mastermind behind the Cottonwood Station robbery was hiding in Buffalo Flat under a new name and identity. But without knowing what that new identity was, they would have to investigate the same way Longarm was, by trying to find men who had moved into the area approximately a decade earlier.

Longarm's gut told him that his thoughts were leading him in the right direction. He didn't have the full story yet, of course, but he felt that if he could find Blaze Harker, everything else would fall into place.

He was so deep in thought that he almost missed the telltale flash of light as the sun reflected off something shiny on the side of a brush-covered hill ahead of him. As he caught that scintillant flash from the corner of his eye, his instincts took over. He kicked his feet loose from the stirrups and went out of the saddle in a rolling dive, grabbing the Henry rifle from the saddle boot as he fell. A gunshot cracked sharply and a bullet whined by somewhere, too close for comfort.

Longarm landed hard but managed to hang on to the rifle. He rolled behind a clump of brush that shielded him from the bushwhacker's view but wouldn't do a damned thing to stop a bullet. He got proof of that as another slug whipped through the branches a few away, searching for him.

From the corner of his eye Longarm spotted a little gully off to his left. He surged up onto his feet and sprinted toward it. A bullet kicked up dirt and gravel at his feet as he threw himself forward. Sprawling in the shallow gully, he hunkered down as low as he could. He was out of the line of fire now, but if he stood up or even raised his head, the bushwhacker would have a clean shot at him again.

This was one hell of a mess, thought Longarm bitterly.

He began to crawl, inching himself along with his elbows and toes. The gully twisted and turned for a couple of hundred yards, maybe farther. If he could work his way around to the other side of that hill, he might be able to get behind the ambusher. More shots rang out, but they were being fired blindly now. The rifleman couldn't see him.

Suddenly a handgun spat several times. The rifle cracked again, then again. Those shots weren't directed at him, Longarm told himself with a frown. There was a gunfight going on, up there where the ambusher had been hidden.

The shooting continued, and Longarm took a chance. From the sound of things, somebody had bushwhacked the bushwhacker. The rifleman was defending himself now, rather than paying any attention to Longarm. The big lawman leaped up and raced back toward his horse, which had run a short distance down the road and then stopped.

The buckskin shied away a little, but Longarm was able to catch hold of the reins. He jammed a foot in the stirrup and swung up into the saddle, then heeled the horse into a run. The road curved around the hill to the left. Longarm veered the buckskin to the right and took off across country, still aiming to get behind the would-be killer.

The buckskin stretched out and ran at an easy gallop, covering ground in a hurry as Longarm circled the hill. Meanwhile the shooting continued, the sharp reports drifting to Longarm's ears through the warm spring air. As he was looking for a trail that would take him to the top of the hill, he heard a great crackling of brush. A horse burst into view, coming, swiftly and recklessly down the slope as its rider twisted around in the saddle to thumb off shots from a six-gun at some pursuit Longarm couldn't see yet.

Longarm saw the man's high-crowned sombrero, though. He was even close enough to see the little decorative balls hanging from the brim and recognize them from his previous encounter with this gunman. Less than twenty-four hours earlier, this man and his late partner had killed Jasper Gammon and tried to kill Longarm.

Tight-reining the buckskin, Longarm lifted the Henry rifle and drew a bead. The Henry blasted and bucked against his shoulder. The big lawman's aim was true. The bushwhacker's horse stumbled as Longarm's bullet drove into its chest.

Longarm hated like the devil to shoot a good horse, but he didn't figure he had any choice. He wanted to capture the sombrero-wearing bushwhacker, not kill him. The son of a bitch couldn't answer any questions if he was dead.

The mortally wounded horse's front legs folded up underneath it, sending the animal crashing to the earth. The bushwhacker sailed through the air, the sombrero coming off his head to go flying off in one direction while the man went the other. He landed hard and rolled over a couple of times. He came up groggily, struggling to his feet, but by the time he made it, Longarm was right there on top of him. Longarm lashed out with the Henry. The barrel thudded against the man's bare head. His knees unhinged and he fell stunned to the ground.

As Longarm dismounted, he heard hoofbeats approaching from up the slope. He worked the Henry's lever, jacking another round into the chamber just in case whoever had jumped the bushwhacker wanted to continue the fight with him.

For a second it looked like that might be the case, as a second rider came tearing out of the brush, revolver in hand. As the newcomer spotted Longarm, the gun swung toward him, but then the rider abruptly tilted the barrel toward the sky and called, "Hold your fire, mister!"

The voice confirmed what Longarm already knew from the curves of the rider's body in jeans and a tight wool shirt, as well as the chestnut curls tumbling out from under a narrow-brimmed Stetson: the bushwhacker had been routed from his hilltop hideaway by a woman.

Longarm kept the Henry ready just in case the gal changed her mind as she trotted closer on a big bay gelding. She holstered the six-gun, though, and then cuffed her hat back so that it hung from the chin strap around her neck. Longarm could see now that she was young, maybe twenty years old, and she rode as if she had spent most of those years in the saddle.

"I see you got the sidewinder," she said as she reined to a stop about a dozen feet away. "Is he dead?"

"Nope, just knocked cold," said Longarm. He added bluntly, "Who are you?"

"I could ask you the same thing," she returned coolly. "I'd be within my rights to do it, too, since you're on Circle F range."

"And you'd be part of the Circle F?" guessed Longarm.

"My father owns this spread," she admitted. "My name is Beth Ferrell."

"Custis Parker," Longarm said with a nod.

Beth Ferrell's brown eyes widened slightly. "The gunman?"

Longarm silently cursed the reputation that seemed to be spreading through the county like wildfire. "I'm not a gunfighter," he said. "Where'd you get that idea?"

"Some of our hands were in Buffalo Flat last night. They said a man named Parker brought in two men that he'd killed in a shootout."

"That ain't exactly the way it happened."

Beth shrugged. "All I know is what I've heard."

Longarm used the rifle to point at the man lying motionless on the ground. "How'd you come to get mixed up in this fight?"

"I was out for a ride and spotted that man hiding on the hill. He looked like he was up to no good, so I snuck up on him to see what he was doing. Then you rode along and he started shooting at you, so I knew he was as big a varmint as he seemed to be." She patted the walnut grips of the Colt that now rested in a black leather holster on her right hip. "So I threw down on him and chased him out of there."

"You're lucky he didn't ventilate you," Longarm pointed out, unable to keep a touch of stern disapproval out of his voice.

Beth Ferrell snorted. "What was I supposed to do, just ride on and let him kill you?"

"Well, I *am* obliged for the help," Longarm admitted.

Beth leaned forward in the saddle and asked, "Why did he ambush you?"

"I ain't exactly sure. He was pards with that fella I had to shoot yesterday afternoon, when they both jumped an old-timer on his way to Buffalo Flat. I came along then sort of like you did today."

That wasn't strictly true, thought Longarm, but, again, it was close enough for government work.

"So he wanted to even the score for his partner," Beth said.

Longarm nodded. "I reckon." He wasn't sure that was the whole story, however. If someone had paid the two hardcases to ambush and kill Jasper Gammon, their employer could have also hired the remaining one to get rid of Longarm. The only person with any reason to do that, though, was Blaze Harker, in whatever new identity Harker had established.

Did that mean that Harker knew who Longarm really was? Not necessarily, the big lawman decided. Even if Harker knew only that Longarm had interfered with the attempt on Gammon's life, that might be enough to make him decide that he didn't want Longarm hanging around Buffalo Flat.

Again, it was a puzzle, and all Longarm could do was to keep moving the pieces around, trying to find some of them that fit together.

Maybe this bushwhacker could give him some more pieces to the puzzle, he thought. Since it was obvious that Beth Ferrell didn't represent a threat, he slid the Henry back into its scabbard attached to the buckskin's saddle and then knelt beside the man he had knocked out. Longarm prodded the man's shoulder and said sharply, "Wake up, mister. You've got some talking to do."

The bushwhacker's head just lolled limply to the side when Longarm shook him.

Longarm frowned and leaned closer. "What the hell?" he muttered. He took hold of the bushwhacker's chin and jerked it back and forth, but there was still no reaction from the man. Longarm reached for his throat and searched for a pulse. When he didn't find one, he exclaimed, "Damn!" He hadn't thought that he'd hit the bushwhacking bastard hard enough to kill him.

"What's wrong?" Beth asked anxiously.

Longarm rolled the bushwhacker onto his side. There in the middle of the man's back was a black hole in his jacket with a dark stain around it. Longarm pulled up the jacket and shirt and saw the bullethole underneath them. The young woman had done more than chase the bushwhacker off the hill; one of her shots had found him and ultimately killed him. The bullet hadn't gone all the way through, and it had taken a few minutes for the wound to prove fatal. That was why Longarm hadn't noticed that the man was hit.

"He's dead," Longarm said disgustedly as he came to his feet. "I figured on asking him some questions, like why he was trying to kill me, but I reckon I could ask all day long without ever getting an answer now."

Beth's eyes were wide. "You mean I . . . I killed him?"

"It sure looks like it."

"But I just . . . I just shot in his general direction . . . to scare him off you, you know . . . I didn't mean to really *kill* him . . ."

With that, her eyes rolled up in her head, she let out a moan, the reins of her horse slipped from her suddenly limp fingers, and she fell out of the saddle, plummeting heavily to the ground.

Chapter 11

Longarm didn't have time to catch the young woman before she fell, but he was close enough to lunge forward and snag the horse's reins before the animal could bolt. He had seen that Beth's right boot was still caught in the stirrup, and she could have been dragged and badly hurt if the horse had stampeded.

Hauling down hard to keep the spooked mount under control, Longarm reached for Beth's ankle with his other hand and freed her foot from the stirrup. Then he led the horse over to a scrubby mesquite and securely tied the reins to the tree. He hurried back to the side of the unconscious young woman.

She didn't seem to be hurt except for a small scrape on her forehead that she had gotten when she landed. She had just fainted from the realization that she had killed a man. Her well-formed breasts rose and fell at a steady rate under the wool shirt she wore. Her face was pale, with twin spots of color on her cheeks. As Longarm hunkered beside her, he loosened the shirt's top button so that she could breathe a little easier. Beth moaned and stirred slightly as consciousness tried to return to her.

The sudden blast of a shot, followed by a swift rataplan

of hoofbeats, made Longarm straighten hurriedly to his feet and whirl around, his hand going to his gun. He eased it away and left the Colt undrawn as he saw the handful of mounted men racing down the road toward him. If he pulled iron now, likely they would shoot first and ask questions later. Keeping his hands in plain sight, he moved a few steps away from Beth, getting her out of the direct line of fire if gunplay broke out.

There hadn't been any more shots after that warning round, however, and although all the newcomers had their guns out, they didn't seem trigger-happy. Dust billowed up from the hooves of their horses as they came to a stop in the road. The rest of the men covered Longarm as the leader, a white-haired, red-faced, middle-aged man dismounted hurriedly and ran over to Beth. He dropped to his knees beside her and grabbed her shoulders.

One of the men pointing guns at Longarm growled, "If you've hurt Miss Beth, you'll swing, you son of a bitch."

"And we won't waste time takin' you into town, neither," put in one of the other cowboys. "There's a cottonwood over yonder that'll do just fine for a hangin' tree."

Longarm forced himself to stay calm, even though having guns pointed at him always rubbed him the wrong way. It wouldn't help the situation if he got riled up now.

"You're making a mistake, boys," he drawled. "The lady's fine. She just fainted and fell off her horse. Anyway, I didn't have anything to do with it." Other than telling her she'd just killed a man, he added silently.

"I think she's all right," the white-haired man called over to the others, turning his head to do so. "She's coming around now."

Beth moaned, shook her head, and then sat up with the older man's help. "Wha . . . what happened?" she asked. Then her confused gaze fell on the nearby body of the dead bushwhacker, and she cried out.

The white-haired man put his arm around her shoulders.

As he leaned closer to her, Longarm saw the resemblance in their faces and concluded that the man was Mitch Ferrell, Beth's father and the owner of the Circle F. "It's all right, darlin'," he told her. "Nothing's gonna happen to you now. Me and the boys are here."

The first cowboy who had spoken to Longarm asked, "What do you want us to do with this fella, boss?"

Ferrell stood up and helped Beth to her feet. Instead of answering the cowboy's question, he asked his daughter, "What happened? Did that bast—that hombre over there hurt you?"

She shook her head, grimacing a little as the motion hurt her. "No, not at all. I . . . I guess I fainted. The last thing I remember is being on my horse."

"He didn't do anything?" Ferrell prodded. "Your shirt's open."

"No. I'm all right, Dad." Beth blushed as she refastened the top button of her shirt.

The cowboy who seemed to be Ferrell's segundo edged his horse over closer to the dead man. "You kill this gent?" he asked Longarm.

"Nope." Longarm nodded toward Beth. "That'd be the lady's doing."

"Watch what you say, you sonuva—" snapped Ferrell. "My daughter wouldn't—"

"Dad," she broke in. "He's telling the truth. I did kill that man."

Ferrell stared at her, as did the segundo and the other cowboys. "What?" Ferrell asked.

"I killed him," Beth repeated, her voice a little stronger now. "I didn't mean to, but I did. I was out riding when I heard shots. I rode over to see what was going on, and that man had ambushed Mr. Parker here. I threw some lead at him to run him off, and one of the shots . . . one of them must have hit him."

Ferrell looked at Longarm. "Parker?"

"That'd be me," said Longarm. "I was riding along the road when that fella tried to bushwhack me. The lady flushed him out while I was circling the hill. I met him at the bottom and shot his horse out from under him. I was trying to take him alive so that I could ask him why he wanted to ventilate me." Longarm shook his head. "Didn't work out that way, though."

"I know you," the segundo said. He was a tall, rawboned young man with a shock of brown hair under his battered, sweat-stained Stetson. "You're the fella who brought those dead bodies into Buffalo Flat last night."

Ferrell grunted and looked at Longarm. "Is that true?"

"No use in denying it," Longarm said.

"Folks seem to have a habit of windin' up dead around you, mister," said Ferrell. "I'm not sure I want you on my ranch."

"I may have been around three corpses," said Longarm, "but I'll only lay claim to one of them." He changed the subject slightly by asking, "Do any of you know who this hombre was?"

The cowboys gathered around to peer down curiously at the dead man. He had a lean, angular, dark-skinned face with a mustache that drooped over the corners of his mouth. One of the men said, "I never seen him before, but he looks like either a Mex or a 'breed."

"And a mean one, too," added the segundo. "That's a knife scar on his face. He's seen more'n his share of trouble."

"He won't be seeing any more," Ferrell said heavily. "I don't know him. Might have seen him around Buffalo Flat, but I ain't even sure about that."

Mutters of agreement came from the other men as they echoed their boss's comment. Longarm said, "Mind if I take a look through his pockets?"

"Help yourself," Ferrell said.

Longarm knelt beside the corpse again, still hoping to learn *something* from the man, dead or not. The bushwhacker's pockets were empty, though, except for four gold double eagles and a tarnished silver crucifix.

"Eighty bucks," mused Longarm as he clinked the coins together in his hand. That was another indication that the man was a hired gun. Some of the blood money would go to the county to bury him; Longarm didn't know or care where the rest of it would wind up.

"Better give that to me," said Ferrell. "I'll give it to Marshal Gibbs."

"Fine with me," Longarm said as he handed over the double eagles. "Reckon you can haul the corpse into town, too?"

"Yeah, I'll send some men out here with a wagon." Ferrell looked narrow-eyed at Longarm. "What about you? Where were you headed when the shooting started?"

"As a matter of fact, I was riding out to the Circle F to see you," Longarm replied.

That answer surprised Ferrell. His bushy white eyebrows lifted. "To see me? What the devil for?"

"Thought you might be hiring," Longarm answered easily.

The segundo snorted. "We don't hire gunfighters on the Circle F," he said acidly.

"Take it easy, Bob," Ferrell said, his voice crisp with irritation. "I do the hiring and firing, remember." The cattleman looked back at Longarm. "That don't mean there's a place on my spread for a man like you, Parker."

Longarm allowed his own irritation to well up at last. "I don't know why everybody's got it in their heads that I'm a gun-thrower," he snapped. "I've done plenty of cowboying in my time. I can make a hand, happen somebody gives me the chance."

Ferrell glowered at him but said reluctantly, "I never turned away a man looking for an honest job without at least giving him a meal. We're not hiring now, Parker, but you can ride on to the ranch with us and have lunch."

Longarm nodded. "I'm obliged for that, anyway." He walked over to his buckskin, which stood nearby, reins dangling on the ground. By the time he'd mounted, Beth Ferrell was back in the saddle, too, as was her father.

"Bob, stay here with that body until I can send some boys back out with a wagon," instructed Ferrell. The segundo frowned darkly, clearly not liking the order, but he nodded in agreement. The others, including Longarm and Beth, started up the road.

Longarm rode next to Ferrell and asked, apparently idly, "How come you and some of your cowboys came riding along just when you did?"

"We were looking for this wayward daughter of mine," Ferrell answered. "She knows she's not supposed to go traipsin' around by her lonesome."

"I don't see why not," said Beth. "I know this ranch like the back of my hand, I can ride as good as any of those wild cowboys you have working for you, and I can handle a six-gun."

"Yeah, I reckon we've seen proof of that," her father said.

Beth glared across at him. "I told you, I didn't mean to kill that man. It was an accident."

"And when you realized you'd done it, you swooned," Ferrell pointed out. "If you'd run across some rustlers, would you have been able to face up to them and use that hogleg you badgered me into giving you?"

"I would have been all right," Beth insisted stubbornly.

Longarm glanced at the holstered pistol on her hip. It was a .38, hardly big enough to be called a hogleg. But he had to admit she had handled it pretty well. Ferrell had a point, though; blazing away at random was a lot different than standing up to somebody who was looking right at you and shooting back.

He said to Ferrell, "Having trouble with rustlers, are you?"

96

The rancher snorted. "When was there a time when a man didn't have trouble with damned cow thieves? Seems like I've had to fight to hang on to what's mine ever since I came to this country. Ten years ago, the Comanches and the Kiowas were still raiding in these parts from time to time, and after they settled down there were whole gangs of owlhoots and wideloopers. These days it's more a matter of a few hardcases driftin' through and helping themselves to some stock every now and then, but it's still a worry."

"Ten years you've been around here, eh?"

"That's right. Well, almost that long. Came out from New Orleans. I used to captain a riverboat, but I got tired of being away from home all the time. I sold the boat and brought Beth and her ma out here to start the ranch." Ferrell's normally rough voice softened a little. "My wife never got to see the place, though. She fell sick on the way and didn't make it."

"Sorry," Longarm said quietly. "Didn't mean to dredge up old memories."

"Well, it's a long time in the past," Ferrell said with a sigh. "And Beth and me have done pretty good for ourselves, I reckon." He squinted at his daughter. "The gal's a mite rough around the edges and headstrong, like a colt that ain't been gentled proper. I reckon that's because her ma wasn't around to see that she grew up lady-like."

"I can be every inch a lady," Beth said coolly, "when I want to."

Longarm imagined that was true. But it was clear that Beth Ferrell had a mind of her own.

It was also clear that once again he was on the wrong trail. Ferrell had a history before coming to Buffalo Flat, and apparently it didn't include holding up trains. There wouldn't have been time for that while he was captaining a riverboat. On the other hand, Longarm had only Ferrell's word for that. It was even possible that Ferrell had lied to his wife and daughter and just pretended to be steaming up and down the Mississippi, while he was really off leading a life of crime. Longarm had already looked at Ferrell's hair, remembering that streak of white that had given Blaze Harker his name. It was possible that the rest of the man's hair had turned white since then, so that the streak blended in.

Longarm said to Beth, "Did you ever travel on that riverboat?"

"Of course," she replied without hesitation. "When I was eight years old I wanted to be a riverboat pilot, just like Mark Twain."

"And now she wants to be a cowboy," said Ferrell with a chuckle. Beth glared at him.

Well, that just about did it, thought Longarm. Unless Beth was in on her father's deception, it seemed highly unlikely that Mitch Ferrell was really Blaze Harker. Not impossible, of course, but Longarm's instincts told him he would be wasting his time by pursuing this angle.

At least he would get a meal out of the trip, he told himself, and he had gotten to meet a pretty girl, even though it hadn't been under very good circumstances.

The group rode on several miles to the headquarters of the Circle F. The ranch house was a large, whitewashed frame structure shaded by cottonwoods and pecan trees. A creek ran nearby, furnishing fresh water. There were a couple of barns, several corrals, a long bunkhouse for the hands, a smokehouse, and several other outbuildings. The place was well kept up and obviously successful. As far as Longarm could see, Ferrell had done a good job with both his ranch and his daughter.

A bearded, limping old cowboy called Flapjack was the cook. He didn't mind that there was a guest for lunch. "Always plenty o' beans in the pot," he greeted Longarm.

The dining room in the house was big, with a long table that would seat all the hands. They ate together, with the food being served by the Mexican woman who was married to Flapjack. It was simple ranch fare, beef and beans and cornbread, along with collard greens and potatoes and for dessert peach cobbler. Longarm ate heartily and enjoyed it.

Before lunch, Ferrell had sent a couple of men with a buckboard to pick up the body of the dead bushwhacker and deliver it into town. When Longarm heard horses outside as they were finishing the meal, he assumed the men were already back from Buffalo Flat, although it didn't seem like there had been time for that. But instead, one of the men got up to look and came back with the news that they had visitors.

"Buggy comin' down the road, boss," the puncher reported to Ferrell. "Man and a woman in it."

Carefully, Longarm kept his face impassive, but he had a sneaking suspicion who these newcomers were.

"Who is it?" asked Ferrell.

"Never saw 'em before," replied the cowboy, "but they're dressed like dudes. I reckon they came out here from town for some reason."

Wanton, redheaded Millie Kyle, thought Longarm, and her so-called husband. Just as he had expected, the money trail had led them to the Circle F ranch, too.

Chapter 12

The morning had been wasted as far as Millie was concerned. She had gone to see Jim Carver, the saddlemaker, using her alleged curiosity about having a sidesaddle made as an excuse for visiting his shop. A middle-aged man with a lined, leathery face, he had flirted shamelessly with her and had been only too happy to tell her in great detail about his life before he came to Buffalo Flat. He had grown up in East Texas, had lived for a time in Waco, and had moved to Buffalo Flat to open his saddle shop nine years earlier. He had a wife and six children, most of whom were grown, and there was a photograph of the entire family, dressed up and stiffly posed, on the wall of the shop. If Carver had led a secret life as a daring bandit, Millie would eat one of the man's saddles.

Salado's visit to the blacksmith shop had been equally fruitless. Barney Rosson had been an apprentice blacksmith in Austin, the state capital, before moving to Buffalo Flat. In and off itself, that might have been a lie, but Rosson had proudly showed Salado a newspaper clipping about how he had stopped a runaway wagon team and saved the life of a state legislator who was about to be trampled. Unless it was a very elaborate hoax, that seemed to establish Rosson's previous life well enough to satisfy Salado.

"That just leaves us with Ferrell," Millie had said on their way out to the Circle F. "If it doesn't pan out that he's the man we're looking for, what then?"

"We keep looking," Salado had replied grimly. "That money *has* to be here somewhere!"

Millie had laughed hollowly. "Either that, or old Claude was lying his fool head off before he died."

That prospect had begun to worry her more and more. What if none of their suspicions were true? If that turned out to be the case, then they had come all this way to Texas for nothing.

But maybe that wasn't so bad, she told herself now as the buggy approached the Circle F ranch house with Salado at the reins. Millie looked around. This part of the country was rugged in places, with quite a few rocky ridges running through it, but there were also wooded hills and broad, lush pastures. It was a lot more pleasing to her eyes than the flatlands of Iowa and Kansas. Maybe she felt that way because she'd had such bad experiences in those other places, but whatever the reason, she found herself thinking that this might not be such a bad place to settle down. She wondered suddenly what it would be like to have a real job, such as working in that dress shop in Buffalo Flat, and to have a real home as well.

They were in sight of the ranch house now. The banker, Charles Stroud, had given them good directions to the place. As Salado brought the buggy to a halt in front of the impressive house, a craggy-faced, white-haired man stepped onto the porch and gave them a polite nod. "Howdy, folks," he said. "Something I can help you with?"

Salado tied the reins around the brake handle and asked, "Would you be Mr. Ferrell, sir?"

The white-haired man nodded. "Yeah, I'm Mitch Ferrell."

"Then this beautiful ranch is your spread," said Salado

with a smile. "Just the man I wanted to talk to. My name is J. Robert Kyle, and this is my wife Mildred."

Ferrell nodded politely and said, "Ma'am," to Millie. He was clearly puzzled by why these two city folks had driven out to his ranch.

"Charles Stroud, who runs the bank in Buffalo Flat, gave me your name and told us how to get out here," Salado went on. "I have a business proposition for you, sir, if you'd care to discuss it . . ."

He moved one foot closer to the edge of the buggy's floorboard, as if he were about to step out. It was an obvious hint for an invitation to light and sit. Ferrell didn't fail to recognize it. He said, "You folks climb down from that buggy and come on in. We're just finishing lunch, but you're welcome to stay. Always plenty of beans in the pot, as my cook Flapjack says."

"Thank you," Salado said. "We'll take you up on that."

He hopped down lithely from the buggy and helped Millie to the ground — not that she really needed the help. She was just as capable as he was. But she was supposed to be some fragile little flower, so she let him act all chivalrous. Salado and Ferrell shook hands, and the rancher ushered them into the house.

There were several cowboys at the table in the dining room. They all stood up and greeted Millie politely and respectfully. That was sure a change, she thought. She was more accustomed to cowboys asking her how much it would cost for a poke and then taking her upstairs to do the poking.

A Mexican woman set a couple of fresh places next to the head of the table. The cowboys drifted out, getting back to work after their midday meal. That left Salado and Millie alone with Mitch Ferrell. "Now," the cattleman said, "what's this about some sort of deal?"

"Right to business, eh?" Salado said with a faint smile.

"I don't mean to be rude," Ferrell assured them, "but

103

there's always more work around a ranch than can be done, so I don't have a lot of time."

"Certainly, I understand. Simply put, Mr. Ferrell, I'm interested in purchasing a share in your ranch."

For a long moment Ferrell just stared at them. Then he began to frown darkly and finally rumbled, "You say Charles Stroud sent you out here?"

Millie was starting to get a little worried by Ferrell's reaction. He looked angry.

"That's right," said Salado. "We spoke to him about possible investments in the area—"

"That boy's an idiot!" Ferrell burst out. "He knows good and well I'd never sell the Circle F or any part of it. At least he ought to know! His pa and I came to this part of the country about the same time, and old Ben Stroud helped me get started here. He knew how I feel about this spread."

Salado was taken aback by the outburst, but as usual he didn't show his true feelings. "I'm sorry, Mr. Ferrell," he said smoothly. "I promise you, I meant no offense—"

Ferrell waved a big, knobby-knuckled hand. "Shoot, I'm the one who ought to be apologizin'. I didn't mean to rear up on my hind legs like a grizzly bear. It's just that this place is mighty special to me. It was supposed to be my wife's new home, but she passed away on the way out here from New Orleans."

Millie thought she saw an opening. She said, "I'm so sorry to hear about your wife, Mr. Ferrell. You say you came here from New Orleans?"

"That's right. We lived there when I was captaining a riverboat on the Mississippi."

Millie exchanged a lightning-quick glance with Salado. Now that Ferrell was talking about his past, Millie intended to keep him doing so. With quiet, deftly feminine questions, she skillfully got the rancher to tell them all about his late wife and his daughter and their life on the river and in New Orleans.

All the time, in the back of her mind, Millie was cursing in disappointment. Another dead end!

"Where's your daughter now?" asked Salado. "Did she marry and move away?"

"Beth married?" Ferrell shook his head. "Shoot, no. She's too stubborn for that just yet." He looked around the room. "She was here just before you folks drove up. I don't know where she got off to. Maybe she's showing that Parker fella around the ranch."

"Parker?" Salado choked out. Millie wished he hadn't reacted quite so strongly, but she couldn't blame him much. She had almost blurted the same thing herself.

Custis Parker had beaten them out here. The man was definitely becoming a thorn in their side. And Millie no longer doubted that he was after that stolen money, too.

It looked like Salado had been right in what he said earlier. Somehow, they had to get rid of Mr. Custis Parker.

"So tell me, Custis—I *can* call you Custis, can't I?—why you really brought me out here to the barn," said Beth Ferrell. "If I didn't know better, I'd say you had something improper in mind. Come to think of it, I *don't* know better. We just met today, after all."

Longarm muttered under his breath. As enjoyable as it was to have a pretty gal flirt with him, right now it was an added complication he didn't need.

"I just felt like taking a walk after that big meal," he said. He rubbed his belly. "Didn't want to bloat up after all them beans." That ought to kill any romantic notions that were flitting around in the air, he thought.

"Nonsense," said Beth bluntly. "When a man grabs a girl's arm and practically drags her out of the house and heads for the barn with her, he has more in mind than a walk. He's thinking of mischief."

Longarm shook his head. "You've got me all wrong, ma'am," he said stubbornly.

To tell the truth, though, a fella would have to be blind or dead not to have a few improper notions when he looked at Beth Ferrell. The jeans and the wool shirt she wore clung enticingly to the curves of her body, and her hair fell in reddish-brown waves to her shoulders and shone in the sunlight that slanted through cracks in the barn roof. She was as pretty a gal as Longarm had seen in quite a while.

Well, not counting Millie Kyle in Buffalo Flat that morning, he amended.

Beth stepped closer to him and said, "You're going to have to prove I'm wrong about you, Mr. Parker." Before he could stop her, she reached up, put her arms around his neck, and pulled his mouth down to hers.

This was sure his day for getting kissed, he thought as his arms instinctively slid around her trim waist. First Millie and now Beth. He was starting to wonder if somebody had pinned a sign to his back without him knowing it, proclaiming this Pucker Up With Custis Long Day. He shoved that crazy thought out of his head and somewhat more gently disengaged from Beth's sweet, warm lips and moved her back a step.

"I hate to bring this up," he said, "but I ain't that much younger than your pa."

"I don't care," she said, a little breathless from passion. "You're the handsomest man who's come around these parts for a long time. And you were mighty nice to me earlier when I was upset."

"You mean after you killed that bushwhacker?" Longarm hoped the blunt statement would dampen her ardor a little.

She bit her lip for a second and then said, "I really didn't mean to do that. But he was trying to kill you, and he wouldn't have wound up dead if he hadn't ambushed you. I'd say it's more his fault than ours."

Longarm couldn't argue with that. He couldn't argue with much of anything, because Beth had her hands on

106

his chest and was moving them around sort of maddeningly . . .

He made one last attempt to talk sense into her. "Your pa or one of the hands could walk in any time."

She shook her head. "The hands have all ridden back out on the range, and Dad's inside with those visitors, whoever they are." She paused and frowned, and for a second Longarm thought she had tumbled to the fact that he had brought her out here so that Kyle and Millie wouldn't see him. Instead she said, "You don't have to worry that you'll be doing anything I haven't done before. I've sparked with boys plenty of times." She lowered her voice to a whisper. "To tell you the truth, Custis, I've done more than spark with a few of them."

Longarm bit back a groan. Beth was making it mighty difficult to do the gentlemanly thing.

She slid closer to him again. "I just want you to kiss me, Custis. Kiss me, and maybe play with me a little."

Lord, she didn't know what she was doing to him. Or maybe she did, the little minx. Longarm bit the bullet and kissed her again.

It was as hot and sweet as the first time. It got even hotter when she grabbed hold of his hand and brought it to her breast. He caressed the firm globe of female flesh through her shirt and felt the nipple hardening against his palm. Earlier, when he'd loosened the top button, he had gotten the impression that she wasn't wearing anything under the shirt. Now he was able to confirm that. His thumb circled and plucked at the firm bud of her erect nipple.

He was growing erect himself, and she must have felt the increasing pressure of his stiffening manhood against her belly. She slipped a hand between them and grasped his shaft. Longarm's left arm was around her waist. He pulled her tighter against him. She moaned, low in her throat, and her lips parted under his. His tongue slid into her mouth and dueled sensuously with her tongue, darting and gliding in a passionate dance.

It was a mighty fine kiss and might have led to more, but no matter how worked up he was, Longarm was too smart to forget that her father and a bunch of ranch hands were relatively close by. Anything else would have to wait for some other time. He finally broke the kiss again and was about to tell her as much when he heard a footstep behind him. Beth glanced over his shoulder, her eyes widening in surprise and fear. She gasped, "No, Bob, don't!"

Longarm pushed her away and started to turn on his own, but before he could a heavy hand fell on his shoulder and jerked him around. He saw a fist coming at his face.

Chapter 13

Instinct took over and jerked Longarm's head to the side so that the punch only grazed his ear. Even though it was a glancing blow, it was still a painful one, and his reflexes made him strike back against the tall, muscular figure looming in front of him. He drove his left into the man's midsection, a short but powerful blow that sunk Longarm's fist wrist-deep in the man's belly. He gasped in pain and started to double over, which brought his chin into perfect position to meet the sharp right cross that Longarm threw next. The man went down, sprawling on the dusty, straw-littered, hard-packed dirt floor of the barn.

"Bob Teague, what the hell do you think you're doing?" Beth shouted at him.

Longarm recognized Ferrell's segundo, who had been left behind to stay with the bushwhacker's body until the wagon arrived to take it to town. Evidently Teague had just gotten back to the ranch and had walked into the barn to put up his horse. A saddled mount stood just inside the doors of the cavernous building. Teague had reacted swiftly and angrily when he saw Beth in Longarm's embrace.

He started to get up, his mouth bloody from Longarm's

109

punch. Longarm held up a hand, palm out, and said, "Hold on there, old son. There's no need for a ruckus."

"The hell there's not," panted Teague. "I saw you attackin' Miss Beth."

"He wasn't attacking me, you fool!" Beth said. "We were just kissing."

"Looked like it was about to turn into more than that," Teague insisted.

"Oh?" she shot back at him. "You mean like what you and I did a while back out in that pasture by Surefire Creek?"

He gaped at her. "Beth, we said we weren't gonna say anything about that!"

"Well, maybe it's time something was said!"

Longarm started to ease away, since the two of them were paying more attention to each other now than they were to him. From the sound of it, they had some things to work out between them that didn't have anything to do with him. He wondered if the Kyles had left yet.

"Wait just a damned minute!" snapped Teague, turning and grabbing Longarm's sleeve. "I'm not through with you, mister."

"I reckon you are," Longarm said coldly. "And I don't like being grabbed, old son."

"I don't give a damn what you like. You think you can waltz in here like you own the place and start pawing a respectable young lady—"

"Bob, I'm not all that respectable," Beth reminded him. "If you remember what happened out there at Surefire Creek, you know I'm not even very interested in being respectable."

"Evidently you ain't," Teague said with a sneer in his voice, "considering how easy you go to whorin' with a fella you just met."

Beth gasped again, in outrage this time. "Why, you self-righteous son of a bitch!" she said. She stepped quickly to-

ward Teague and swung a hard punch to his jaw, taking
him by surprise. The blow landed solidly and knocked him
back into Longarm. Teague would have fallen again if
Longarm hadn't been there to catch him.

"I reckon maybe you said the wrong thing," Longarm
advised him dryly.

Teague growled a curse. Unable to bring himself to
strike back against a woman, he did the only thing he could
to release his pent-up fury. He twisted suddenly and tack-
led Longarm. Both of them went down hard.

This was getting damned tiresome, thought Longarm.
Teague tried to knee him as they grappled on the barn
floor. Longarm turned his hips so that he took the blow on
his thigh. At the same time, Teague hooked punches to
Longarm's midsection. The big lawman grabbed his shoulders and heaved him to the side, sending Teague rolling
across the ground. Figuring that the Circle F segundo
wasn't going to give up, Longarm went after him. He came
down with a knee in the middle of Teague's back, pinning
him to the ground. He grabbed Teague's right wrist and
twisted that arm up behind the man's back, holding him
helpless. Teague yelped in pain as muscles and tendons
stretched.

A wildcat landed on Longarm's back. "Let go of him!"
Beth cried in his ear. Somehow, Longarm wasn't surprised.
Beth evidently had a pretty volatile nature, and that was
putting it mildly.

He let go of Teague to reach up with both hands and
take hold of Beth's shirt. As he bent forward, he heaved so
that she came up and over him. She let out a yell that
turned into a grunt as she landed on Teague. The impact
knocked the breath out of both of them. They lay there tangled up with each other, gasping for air, as Longarm stood
up and backed away from them.

"What the hell's goin' on here?" roared Mitch Ferrell as
he strode through the open doors of the barn. Flapjack was

111

behind him—and so were Robert and Mildred Kyle. Longarm muttered a curse under his breath when he saw them.

They pretty much ignored him, though, so if that was the way they wanted to play the hand, that was fine with him. He acted like he had never seen them before, either.

"Bob, damn it, quit rollin' around on the ground with my daughter!" ordered Ferrell. "Beth, quit that!" The rancher looked at Longarm. "Parker, what's your part in this?"

Before Longarm could answer, Bob Teague said, "He was molestin' Miss Beth! I caught him in here puttin' his hands all over her!"

Ferrell glowered at Longarm. "Is that true?"

"Your daughter kissed me," replied Longarm coolly. "You said yourself she's a mite headstrong, Ferrell. When she gets a notion, it's hard to talk her out of it."

"You didn't even try to talk me out of it!" Beth accused as she stood up and started brushing straw and dust off her clothes. "You sure didn't fight back any, either!"

Ferrell stepped up to her and took her arm. "You get in the house, girl," he commanded as he pushed her toward the barn doors. "You've always been wild. I reckon that's my fault."

"You don't know how wild I am!" she snapped at him.

Ferrell sighed. "We'll talk about that later." He turned his attention to Teague and asked shrewdly, "How come you to jump Parker, Bob? Were you protecting Beth . . . or were you just jealous?"

Teague flushed. "I think the world of Miss Beth, boss. You know that."

"Maybe you think a little too much of her. We'll talk about that later, too." Ferrell turned to Longarm again. "That leaves you, Parker."

"I'm what you call an innocent bystander in all this, Ferrell," drawled the big lawman. "I didn't mean to cause any trouble."

"But it's got a habit of followin' you around anyway, doesn't it?"

Longarm shrugged. It wouldn't do any good to deny Ferrell's statement. Anyway, he was through here. He had found out what he wanted to know, and he was back where he had started from, with still no idea where Blaze Harker and all that loot from the Cottonwood Station holdup might be.

"I told you I didn't have a job for you," Ferrell went on. "I reckon it'd be best if you headed on back to Buffalo Flat now."

Longarm nodded. "I'll get my horse." He strode past the Kyles, giving them a curt nod as he left the barn. They still ignored him, but Longarm caught the cold-eyed glance Kyle shot at him as he went by.

The buckskin was tied to a hitching post in front of the ranch house. Longarm jerked the reins loose, grabbed the horn, and swung up into the saddle. He had just settled down on the leather when the front door of the house opened and Beth Ferrell hurried out onto the porch.

"Custis!" she called. "Don't go yet!"

Longarm frowned at her. "Ain't you caused enough trouble yet, Miss Ferrell?"

She got a coy look on her face. "Don't you think after what we did in the barn you ought to call me Beth?"

"What we did in the barn didn't really amount to a whole lot," Longarm pointed out, "especially since it appears that you and young Teague are a mite more than friends."

She blushed. "Bob spoke out of turn. That's between him and me."

"Damn right it is. I don't have any part in it and don't want any."

Beth's chin lifted defiantly. "You wanted me," she declared. "I know that. I *felt* it."

Longarm's teeth gritted together. He forced them apart

113

and said, "Keep talking like that and your pa will go get his shotgun for sure."

Her defiance fell away and now she looked genuinely apologetic as she said, "I'm sorry, Custis. I never meant to cause trouble for you. I know you and Dad and everybody else are right. I'm too stubborn, too impulsive. I don't know why I'm that way, but I am."

"You just need to grow up a mite," said Longarm.

She nodded. "I know. Anyway, I wanted to tell you I was sorry for jumping you the way I did when you were wrestling with Bob. I just lost my head when I saw you were hurting him."

"Maybe that's because you care for him more than you thought you did."

Her brown eyes widened in surprise. "You think so? Bob's a nice boy, but . . ."

"He's more than a boy," Longarm pointed out. "He's a man, and he's got a man's feelings. He maybe takes things a mite seriously than you do, Beth. You think on that."

"I . . . I will." She came to the edge of the porch and added softly, "Thank you, Custis."

Longarm just nodded and wheeled the buckskin. He didn't look back as he rode away from the Circle F. Given the generally sordid and violent life he had led, he was a fine one to go around dispensing advice like some wise old uncle, he told himself with a wry grin.

The grin disappeared as he pondered everything that had happened today. He and the Kyles were running around each other in circles, and although he was now certain in his own mind that somehow they knew about the money and were looking for it, too, he didn't know how else they tied into this business. Nor was he any closer to finding Blaze Harker. All he had really accomplished was getting kissed by a couple of pretty girls. Well, that and getting shot at by a no-good bushwhacker. That was another example of his bad luck. If one of Beth's shots hadn't accidentally struck that ambusher, Longarm might have the answers he needed by now.

He was about halfway back to Buffalo Flat when he noticed the clouds building up to the northwest. They were dark blue shading to downright black. Longarm had been in Texas in the springtime before. He knew how fast violent thunderstorms could blow in. As he heeled the buckskin into a slightly faster pace, he saw lightning flicker in the distant clouds and heard a faint rumble of thunder. He wanted to get back to town before the storm hit.

It quickly became obvious that he wasn't going to be able to make it. A cool, almost cold wind began to blow, whipping the branches of the trees back and forth and stirring up little dust devils in the road. Longarm saw more dust ahead of him and realized after a moment that it wasn't being whipped up by the wind. Instead it came from a buggy that was being driven quickly back toward town. Longarm frowned. That couldn't be the Kyles' buggy in front of him. He had left the Circle F before they did, and they hadn't passed him. This was somebody else who was out and about on what was rapidly turning into a stormy afternoon.

He nudged the buckskin into a run, thinking that he would catch up to the buggy and see if the driver needed any help. It took him only a few minutes to draw even with the vehicle. The clouds had obscured the sun by now, casting a gloomy pall over the landscape, and the shadows were thick enough under the buggy's canopy that Longarm couldn't get a good look at the driver at first. He saw a woman's hands clinging rather desperately to the reins, though, struggling to keep the two-horse team under control. The team wasn't actually stampeding, but Longarm could tell that the approaching storm had the animals spooked.

"Hang on!" he called to the driver. He moved up alongside the team and leaned to the side in the saddle to grab the harness of the left-hand horse. He hauled back and brought the team to a halt. Turning toward the buggy, he said over the rising wind, "Give 'em a minute or two to calm down, and then they ought to be all right."

"Thank you," the woman said fervently. "I was afraid they were going to get away from me."

Longarm could see her better now, and he recognized her sleek blond beauty. "Miss Wilkes, ain't it?" he said.

She nodded. "That's right. Have we met, sir?" Before Longarm could answer, she went on, "Wait a minute. Of course, in the bank this morning. You're Mr. Parker. You were talking to Charles."

Longarm smiled. "That's right. Pardon my asking, ma'am, but what are you doing out here all by your lonesome?"

"I was just out for a drive. I often drive around the countryside, especially at this time of year. I love the fresh air."

Longarm could understand that.

"But then that storm started to come up, and I thought I ought to get back to town as quickly as I could," continued Karen Wilkes. She looked at the blackening sky. "I don't think I'm going to make it, though."

"I was on my way back, too. I'll ride along with you, if you don't mind."

"Certainly not. In fact, if you'd like to tie your horse on to the back of the buggy, you can get in here with me, so you'll have at least a little protection from the elements." Karen gave a little laugh. "And perhaps I could talk you into handling the reins, as well."

That sounded like a good idea to Longarm. He said as much as he dismounted and tied the buckskin's reins to the back of the buggy. He stepped up easily to the seat, where Karen moved over to give him room. She handed him the reins.

"I appreciate this, Mr. Parker."

"And I appreciate the ride," Longarm told her. He flapped the reins and called out to the team, getting the horses moving again. The buckskin clopped along behind.

They had gone less than half a mile when the storm hit.

Chapter 14

Fat drops of rain pelted heavily against the black canvas canopy. The wind blew some of them inside the vehicle, and they struck Longarm's legs with stinging force, even through his trousers. "Oh, my Lord!" Karen exclaimed over the roar of the wind as lightning flashed, but if she said anything else it was drowned out by the sudden boom of thunder.

Longarm kept the reins tight so that the horses couldn't bolt. Beside him, Karen turned on the seat to rummage around in the boot behind them. The move made her thigh press hard against his, and Longarm felt the heat of her flesh even through two layers of clothing. When she faced forward again, she was holding a bright yellow slicker.

"I thought I remembered there was one of these behind the seat," she said, still speaking loudly so she could be heard over the storm. "I'll spread it over our legs!"

The slicker covered their legs fairly well, and there was something intimate about sharing its protection, Longarm thought. The wind still blew in enough rain so that Longarm's shirt was dampened. The temperature had dropped quite a bit in a short period of time. Karen huddled against his side, evidently seeking warmth. Longarm would have put an arm around her to comfort her, but he needed both hands on the reins.

As the storm grew more violent, Longarm began to worry that a cyclone might come swooping down out of the clouds. This part of the country was plagued by tornadoes during the spring. If that happened, he and Karen would have to look for a ditch or a gully in which to take shelter, and they wouldn't have any time to waste, either. A cyclone was one of the quickest-striking, most destructive forces of nature known to man.

The team was getting more and more fractious. Longarm bit back curses as he struggled to keep the horses under control. Lightning flashed and thunder boomed and the wind howled. It was still several miles to Buffalo Flat, Longarm estimated, and he didn't know if they could make it that far in this storm or not.

Suddenly, with a crack that sounded like the heavens being torn asunder, a huge pecan tree to the side of the road in front of them split halfway up the trunk under the ferocious pounding of the wind. The upper half of the tree fell across the road with a massive crash. Longarm hauled back sharply on the reins just in time to prevent the team from running into the fallen tree.

"My God!" cried Karen. "If we'd been a little farther on, that would have crushed us!"

Longarm nodded grimly. "It sure would have. I think we better hunt some place to ride out this storm. It probably won't last too long, but it's getting too dangerous for us to be out in it!"

"I . . . I don't know of anywhere—Wait! I've been to a place . . . I don't think it's too far from here . . . There's an overhanging bluff that forms an area almost like a cave!"

"Can you find it?"

"I think so!" Karen looked around, trying to orient herself. "You'll have to turn the buggy around and go back the way we came!"

That was all right with Longarm, as long as it got them to some shelter. Following Karen's directions, he drove about half a mile back toward the Circle F. Then she pointed and said, "Head for that ridge over there!"

Longarm left the road and started across country. It wasn't easy going, considering that the downpour had made the ground soft and muddy. He had to get out a couple of times and put his shoulder to the back of the buggy so that he could give it a shove and get it through the worst spots, while Karen handled the reins. By the time they reached the ridge, he was soaked to the skin.

"That way!" she said. "Follow the ridge!"

Longarm did so, and after a few minutes they came to a tall limestone bluff that overhung a stretch of rocky ground underneath it. Longarm drove under the overhang, and to his relief the beetling cliff blocked both the wind and the rain, although a few drops still swirled into the protected area from time to time.

"Thank God!" said Karen. "I didn't know if we were going to make it or not."

"Neither did I," admitted Longarm. "Stay here while I see about tying up those horses."

Some scrub brush grew out of the stony ground at the base of the bluff. Longarm tied the reins of the team to a sturdy-looking bush and left the buckskin hitched to the back of the buggy. He climbed into the vehicle again and sat down next to Karen.

"I reckon we'll be more comfortable in here than we would on that rocky ground out there," he said.

She agreed. "It's not too bad in here now, but I'm still cold."

"I'd say that we could huddle up for warmth—meaning no disrespect, of course, ma'am—but as wet as I am, I ain't sure it'd do any good."

121

"Oh, shoot," she said as she moved closer to him. "I'm pretty well soaked, too." She put her head against his shoulder. Her thick blond hair brushed the side of his face.

This was sure his day for cuddling up with good-looking women, thought Longarm. He couldn't recall when he'd had his arms around three such pretty gals in such a short span of time. Karen was so close to him that he could feel the rhythm of her breathing. It was rapid at first, especially when lightning struck somewhere close by with a crackle and the thunder that followed hard on the heels of the flash was deafening. But as the time went by, she settled down. Her breaths steadied and deepened until Longarm knew she had gone to sleep with her head on his shoulder.

After a while he dozed off himself, with the smell of Karen's hair and the warmth of her body filling his senses. A buggy seat wasn't the most comfortable place in the world, but it had been a busy day.

He wasn't sure how long he slept . . . long enough to get a stiff neck, that was for sure. He sat up a little and moved his other shoulder and his neck, trying to loosen the muscle but being careful not to awaken Karen. He wasn't successful in either of those things. She lifted her head from his shoulder and murmured, "Oh, my. I . . . I must have dozed off."

"I reckon we both did," Longarm told her. He looked out and saw that the rain was still falling, although the wind wasn't as strong now and the thunder and lightning were more distant. "Looks like the storm's letting up a little. We might be able to make it to town now."

He felt a shudder go through her. "Not yet," she said. "I didn't like that. I'd rather stay here until it's all over."

Longarm didn't know what time it was, but he figured it was still early enough so that they could wait a while and still get back to Buffalo Flat before night fell. He went to move the arm that was around her shoulders, but she reached up and laid her hand on his.

"Leave it there," she said. "It feels good."

Longarm didn't mind. When he moved his head a minute later, though, a twinge went through that stiff neck muscle, and Karen must have felt the little jerk of reaction that he gave. She straightened a little and asked, "What's wrong?"

"This neck of mine is a mite stiff," replied Longarm. "Reckon I must've slept on it wrong when I dozed off."

"Because you were holding me, I imagine." She sat up even more. "Turn a little. I can fix a stiff neck."

"You don't have to —"

"It's entirely possible that you saved my life, Mr. Parker. I think I can rub your neck."

Longarm wasn't going to argue with her, and as soon as he felt the touch of her slender fingers, he was glad that he hadn't. She was stronger than he would have guessed that a town girl would be, and her hands skillfully stroked and massaged his neck until the stiff muscle relaxed and she had rubbed the soreness right out of it.

"That feels mighty good now," he said as he turned back toward her.

She put her hands on the back of his neck from this direction and rubbed gently, the fingertips moving in circles. Their faces were only a few inches apart. In the shadows under the bluff, he couldn't see her all that well, but he felt the warmth of her breath on his face.

Longarm thought, *You don't suppose* . . .

Sure enough, she leaned forward and kissed him.

That made three out of three. Every woman he'd met today had given him a big smooch. Karen Wilkes stacked up just fine against Millie Kyle and Beth Ferrell in that department, too. Her lips were full and warm and eager. They parted without any urging on his part. In fact, her tongue slid into his mouth first, before he could even begin to explore hers.

Longarm's arms went around her and pulled her closer to him. She wore the same dark blue outfit she'd had on earlier in the day, but it was still damp now and clung to her body, which made it that much easier for her to mold herself against him. He felt himself responding to the insistent pressure of her breasts against his chest and the tantalizing way her tongue darted against his.

It cost him an effort, but he managed to take his lips away from hers and say, "Miss Wilkes, I pure-dee hate to do this, but I got to remind you that you're engaged to be married—"

"No, I'm not," she said.

Longarm frowned. "But when Mr. Stroud introduced us—"

"Charles Stroud is a very arrogant man. He decided that we should be married, and he assumed that I would go along with that. I've made him no promises, though, except in his own mind."

"And that doesn't count for anything?"

"No," she answered without hesitation. "It doesn't."

"Well, then," mused Longarm, "in that case . . ."

He kissed her this time.

Karen responded eagerly, especially when Longarm moved a hand to her right breast and cupped it through her dress. She reached down and pressed her hand against his erection through his trousers. It took her only a moment to unfasten the buttons, reach inside, and free his shaft from its confinement. As the long, thick pole sprang free, she tried to close her hand around it but failed. "My God, Mr. Parker!" she gasped. "There certainly is a lot of you."

"Custis," he told her. "Considering how well-acquainted we're getting, I reckon it'd be better if you called me Custis."

She smiled. "I agree." Then she leaned over and pressed

124

her lips to the head of his rock-hard organ. She looked up and asked, "Do you like that . . . Custis?"

She didn't wait for an answer. Instead she bent to the task again and opened her lips to take the whole head into her mouth.

Karen had just moved ahead of Millie and Beth on points, he thought. Not that it was really a competition. Still, given the fluency with which she spoke French, he wouldn't have wagered against her.

For long moments, he leaned back against the buggy seat and luxuriated in what she was doing to him. He didn't think about the fact that they were wearing damp, somewhat uncomfortable clothing or that they barely knew each other. Karen was obviously drawn to him with an attraction so powerful that it would not be denied. For his part, he was enough of a gentleman that he usually steered clear of married women or even ones who were engaged, but it wouldn't have been very chivalrous of him not to believe her when she said she wasn't planning to marry Charles Stroud, now would it? Given the circumstances and the way she seemed to be trying to swallow as much of his pole as possible, there wasn't a damned thing he could do except sit back and enjoy it.

Eventually she gave him a final licking from base to tip and sat up. "You do make a girl's jaw ache a little, Custis," she said.

"Sorry."

"Don't be," she said with a smile. "It was more than worth it." She held his manhood with both hands, slowly stroking her palms up and down on it. "I want more, though, if you're up to it . . . and I can see for myself that you are."

"Don't tease me, woman," he growled.

"All right. No teasing." She took her hands off him and lifted her skirts around her waist. Longarm saw all sorts of silky, feminine frippery under there, but Karen managed to get enough of it out of the way so that when she swung a leg over him and straddled him on the wagon seat, the head of his shaft touched bare, slick, heated flesh. He felt the tickle of the fine-spun hair that surrounded her opening as she began to slide slowly down onto him. He let her set the pace, even though he wanted to thrust up into her and sheath himself all the way. They got there soon enough, as she settled down until he was all the way inside her.

She wrapped her arms around his neck and just sat there for a long moment, fully impaled on his shaft. She was breathing rapidly and shallowly, and she gave a little whimpering moan deep in her throat. "So big," she murmured. "You fill me up so much . . ."

As if they both sensed the need at the same instant, they began to move. Longarm thrust up while Karen pumped her hips to meet him. He kissed her cheeks, her nose, her eyes, and finally her mouth. This time when her lips parted his tongue slid between them and delved deeply into her mouth, just as his manhood was penetrating deep into her femininity.

As she began to buck harder against him, Longarm slipped his hands underneath her hips to steady her. They would both be mighty disappointed if she took a tumble off of him right now. As they came together with each thrust, her pelvis ground against his. In the distance, a long peal of thunder rolled over the soaked landscape, a fitting accompaniment to the passion that was building in the buggy. The vehicle began to rock on its springs.

Longarm felt his climax building up, knew he couldn't last much longer, knew Karen didn't want him to. She cried out again and began to shudder as her own culmination rippled through her. That sent Longarm over the edge. He emptied himself inside her, his seed boiling out in white-hot bursts.

They topped the peak together and held on tightly to each other as they went down the far side of the crest.

Karen's shudders finally died away. Both of them were breathless. Longarm felt his heart pounding in his chest and could feel hers thudding heavily as well. He kissed her neck and stroked her back. She murmured his name.

Finally, his organ slipped out of her, and she lifted her head to say, "I don't think we should tell anyone about this."

"I ain't the sort of fella who likes to brag about such things, ma'am," Longarm assured her.

"Oh, for goodness' sake, don't call me ma'am anymore." She laughed. "That's just silly."

"Yeah," agreed Longarm with a grin. "I reckon it is. But you don't have to worry about me keeping this quiet. I figure it ain't anybody's business but ours."

"That's exactly the way I feel about it."

And by doing that, she kept her options open, he thought somewhat cynically. Just because she hadn't agreed to marry Charles Stroud just yet didn't mean that she wouldn't say yes someday.

They straightened themselves up and rearranged their clothes. The rain had tapered off even more to a steady drizzle, but the sky was still thickly overcast and gloomy. Longarm said, "I'll take a look around and see how muddy the ground is. I think we can get out of here and start on back to town now."

"Yes, that would be a good idea," Karen said.

Longarm dropped down from the buggy and checked on the horses first thing. All three of them were all right. He walked to the edge of the rocky ground under the overhang of the bluff and looked out on the rain-soaked landscape.

The crack of the shot and the whine of the bullet past his ear sounded at the same time.

Chapter 15

Longarm heard the slug hit the face of the limestone bluff. Karen cried out in alarm, but he knew she wasn't hit. "Get behind the buggy!" he called to her as he wheeled and lunged around the back of the vehicle, ducking under the buckskin's reins.

He got there in time to catch Karen as she scrambled and half-fell out of the buggy. He told her to stay low and then hurried over to his mount to pull the Henry rifle out of its sheath. As he did so, another shot whipped in, this time striking the buggy itself and ricocheting off with a high-pitched whine.

Longarm levered a round into the Henry's chamber and brought the rifle to his shoulder. He hadn't spotted the bushwhacker yet, but he fired anyway, worked the Henry's lever, and fired again. He wanted the son of a bitch to know that he was going to put up a fight. Then he crouched at the rear corner of the buggy, his keen eyes searching the drenched landscape.

The next time the ambusher's rifle cracked, Longarm saw a puff of smoke from a grove of pecan trees about eighty yards away. At the same time, one of the horses hitched to the buggy let out a shrill scream and slumped to the side, blood spouting from a wound in its neck. Karen screamed, too.

"Custis, he's killing the horses!"

Longarm saw that and knew that if the bushwhacker shot down all three of the animals, he and Karen would be stuck here. He stepped out from behind the buggy and grabbed the buckskin's reins. He couldn't do anything to help the other horse in the team, but he might be able to keep the bushwhacker from killing the buckskin.

He felt as much as heard the wind-rip of another slug passing close beside his ear as he jerked the reins loose. Then he fell back again, pulling the buckskin with him behind the buggy. He thrust the reins into Karen's trembling hands and said, "Hang on to him!" The buggy wasn't big enough to completely protect the buckskin, but it was better cover than nothing.

A moment later, the bushwhacker shot and killed the other buggy horse. Karen jerked and whimpered as the animal was hit and went down next to its luckless partner in harness.

"Who's out there?" she asked, her voice taut with fear. "Who's trying to kill us?"

Longarm already had asked himself the same question. One thing was certain, and one thing only: this ambusher wasn't the sombrero-wearing hardcase who tried to kill him earlier in the day. That bastard was dead. Other than him, the bushwhacker could be almost anybody he had met since coming to Buffalo Flat, thought Longarm, or even somebody who was a stranger to him.

He edged the barrel of the Henry around the back of the buggy and threw another shot at the pecan trees. If he could stand off the unknown gunman until night fell in an hour or so, then he and Karen might be able to make a break for it on the buckskin.

Then things began to look even grimmer as one of the

bushwhacker's slugs ricocheted off the bluff behind them and glanced off one of the buggy wheels with a loud *spang*! So far the hidden gunman's bullets hadn't bounced when they hit the bluff. That one must have found a particularly hard stone that caused it to ricochet instead of digging in. But if it had happened once it could happen again, and if the rifleman poured enough lead in . . .

Longarm knew they couldn't afford to wait. He and Karen had to get out of this trap now.

"I don't see why we couldn't have waited until the rain stopped completely," Millie complained as the buggy rolled along the road. The mud sucked at the wheels, but Salado seemed confident that as long as they kept moving, they wouldn't bog down.

"Because we were wasting our time there," he snapped. "Ferrell doesn't have anything to do with that money. You heard what he said about being a riverboat captain before he came to Texas."

"He could have been lying," Millie pointed out.

Salado waved that away. "I don't think so," he said disgustedly. "He was just as believable as everybody else we've talked to in Buffalo Flat."

"Well, somebody's lying. The money *has* to be here."

"We just haven't found the right person yet." Salado snorted. "Anyway, it was too tense out there at the Circle F. The place was getting in my nerves, and so was the way Ferrell and his daughter kept arguing with each other. I never would have stayed as long as we did if Ferrell hadn't insisted there was a bad storm coming."

"And sure enough, there was," said Millie. "I'm glad we weren't out in that."

Salado shrugged. "I suppose you're right." He flicked the reins and urged the buggy team on through the light rain. "Now, we've got to figure out what that bastard Parker has to do with all this. I don't trust him. If he keeps dogging our trail, I swear I'm going to shoot him."

You might try, thought Millie, remembering the easy way Parker moved, which indicated that he had speed and grace to spare. *But I'm not sure you'd succeed* . . .

"Ferrell said he just came out there looking for a job," she reminded Salado.

"And you believed that?" He snorted in contempt. "That may be what he told Ferrell, but we both know that it's not true. There's no such thing as a coincidence, Millie."

She wasn't sure she believed that, but Salado was probably right in Parker's case. She thought he was after the money, too.

"It must be nice, having a family that cares about you," she murmured, abruptly changing the subject.

Salado glanced over at her. "What? What are you talking about?"

"Beth Ferrell."

"Are you joking? Her father was furious at her. I think she's been screwing that cowboy Teague."

"Ferrell yells at her because he's worried about her," said Millie. "That means he loves her. I never had a family like that."

He gave her an ugly grin. "From what you've told me, that uncle of yours loved you plenty."

She didn't know whether to cry or yell in anger at that. She punched him on the arm. "Shut up!" she said miserably. "I never should have told you about that, you . . . you . . ."

"Hey, take it easy! I didn't mean anything by it!"

"Then you shouldn't have said it!"

He hauled back on the reins, slowing the buggy. "Look, Millie—"

Whatever he had been about to say went unsaid as shots began to crash somewhere not too far ahead along the road.

132

Salado yanked the team to a halt and sat up straight on the buggy seat. "What the hell!" he exclaimed.

"It's some sort of gunfight," Millie said. "Turn around, and let's get out of here!"

"Wait a minute. I want to know what's going on."

"What's going on is that somebody is trying to kill somebody else, and we don't need to be in the middle of it!" She tugged at his arm, trying to get him to turn the buggy around, but he shook her off.

"We're going to see what this is about." With that, he slapped the reins on the backs of the horses and sent them trotting ahead.

Millie knew she would be wasting her breath to argue with him. Once he got an idea in his head, nothing could persuade him otherwise. But if he was bound and determined to go barging into trouble, she would at least be ready for it. She reached into her bag and took out the little pistol she always carried. Unfortunately, those sounded like rifles banging away at each other up there, so a handgun might not do much good.

The buggy wheeled around a bend in the trail. A couple of hundred yards off to the left rose a sheer limestone bluff. A grove of pecan trees was between the road and the bluff. Millie spotted a horse tied at the edge of the trees, standing in the rain with its head down. With all the mist in the air, she couldn't be sure, but she thought she saw a cloud of powdersmoke floating over the trees. The shots were definitely coming from that direction.

Millie made one last try as Salado halted the buggy. "Let's get out of here," she urged. "Whatever's going on here, it's none of our business."

For a moment she thought he was going to agree with her, but then he drew his pistol and said, "No, I'm going to see who's in those trees."

"You'll get yourself killed!"

He grinned confidently. "You forget who you're talking to. I can handle myself just fine."

He handed the reins to Millie, then stepped down from the buggy and started toward the trees on foot. She watched him for a few seconds and then angrily tied the reins around the brake lever. Holding her own pistol, she jumped down from the buggy and hurried after him.

Salado heard her coming. Her shoes made squishing sounds in the mud. He turned, grimaced at her, and waved her back. Stubbornly, Millie ignored him and came on.

"What are you doing?" he hissed at her as she caught up to him.

"The same thing you're doing," she snapped. "If it's not crazy for you to do it, then it's not crazy for me, either."

He rolled his eyes. "Go back to the buggy."

"Go to hell." She strode on past him, heading for the pecan trees.

Salado had no choice but to go with her. As they approached the trees, he whispered, "Split up. I'll go left, you go right."

Millie nodded her agreement. They veered apart, circling a little so that they could come at the trees from two different angles.

Millie's heart pounded in her chest. She had been in dangerous situations before, of course, but she had never waltzed into one like this of her own volition. She knew Salado was a hunch player, though, and he must have a hunch that this was important somehow. If only it didn't get one or both of them killed . . .

She reached the trees and slid into them. There wasn't much undergrowth. Moving as silently as possible from tree trunk to tree trunk, she closed in on the sound of shots. After a moment she spotted a man in a long duster, with his hat pulled low over his face, aiming a rifle at the bluff. Millie shifted her position a little so that she could see what the man was shooting at. She spotted a buggy parked next to the bluff. That seemed to be the gunman's target. Both of the horses hitched to the buggy were down, evidently shot and killed by the man in the duster. Someone was behind the buggy, maybe two people, Millie couldn't be sure. And another horse. The rifleman sure had them pinned down.

Salado stepped into sight on the far side of the gunman, leveled his pistol at the man, and called, "Hold it, mister! Drop that rifle!"

Instead of complying with the order, the bushwhacker turned sharply, dropped to one knee, and fired the rifle. Salado let out a yell, whether of surprise or pain Millie couldn't tell and returned the fire.

With her partner in trouble, Millie did the only thing she could. She started shooting, too.

Longarm frowned in surprise as he heard the sudden burst of shots in the grove of trees where the bushwhacker lurked. What sounded like a couple of pistols had opened up, too, but the shots didn't seem to be coming at the bluff. From the sound of it, for the second time today a bushwhacker had had the tables turned on him.

Longarm turned to Karen and asked, "Can you use a rifle?"

"I . . . I've shot one a time or two in my life," she answered.

He thrust the Henry into her hands. She gasped a little at the weight of it. "There are still quite a few rounds in it," Longarm told her. "You can rest the barrel on the buggy to steady it if you have to fire. If anybody comes at you that you don't know and looks like they mean you harm, don't hesitate to shoot them."

"Where are you going?"

"To see if I can get around those trees. It sounds like whoever was shooting at us has some trouble of his own now. I'd like to add to it."

With that he swung up into the buckskin's saddle and drove his heels into the horse's flanks. The buckskin lunged out from behind the buggy. Longarm knew it was hard to hit a man on a running horse. He sent the buckskin galloping at an angle that would take him around the trees.

Longarm drew his Colt as the shots tapered off in the grove of pecan trees and then stopped completely. He rode around the end of the grove in time to see a man carrying a rifle and running toward a tied horse. The stranger wore a long duster that flapped as he ran, and a broad-brimmed black hat was pulled down over his eyes so that Longarm couldn't see his face. He jerked the reins loose and vaulted into the saddle. The Colt bucked in Longarm's hand as the big lawman sent a warning shot over the man's head. "Hold it!" Longarm bellowed.

The man ignored him and put the spurs to the horse. With a squeal, it lunged ahead. The man bent low over the horse's neck, making himself a smaller target. Longarm squeezed off a couple more shots, but the running horse didn't falter. The range was a little too much for accurate shooting with a handgun, even for an expert like Longarm.

He might have given chase, but at that moment another figure stumbled out of the trees and ran toward him. Longarm's eyes widened in surprise as he recognized the lithe shape and the red hair belonging to Millie Kyle. "Help us!" she cried as she leaped out to grab the buckskin's harness. "Oh, my God! Salado's been shot!"

Longarm wasn't sure who Salado was. Millie's nickname for her husband, maybe? At any rate, he couldn't just gallop off and leave a half-hysterical woman and a wounded man behind. Whoever Salado was, he might be badly hurt.

He dismounted, whipped the buckskin's reins around a sapling, and grabbed Millie's arms. She was sobbing and muttering, and Longarm gave her a little shake and said, "Settle down! What's going on here?"

"B-back there!" Millie managed to gasp out as she pointed with her free hand into the trees. "He's been shot!"

"Show me," Longarm told her.

He kept his gun out as she led him deeper into the trees. He didn't know what he was going to find in here, but whatever it was he didn't want to face it without iron in his hand.

Millie stopped short and looked around in what appeared to be genuine confusion. "Where is he?" she said. "He was right here a minute ago!"

"What happened?" asked Longarm. "Who's hurt?"

"My . . . my husband," she said, confirming Longarm's suspicion. "R-Robert. I . . . I call him Salado, because that's where he's from."

Made sense, Longarm supposed. But it didn't answer the question of where Kyle—an allegedly wounded Kyle—had gotten off to.

He didn't have to wait long to find out the answer. A voice behind him said coldly, "Hold it, Parker! Try anything funny and I'll blow your damned brains out."

Chapter 16

Longarm had been threatened enough times in his career so that he knew when a man meant it. He recognized as well the particular edge in a man's voice that said the threat was backed up by a gun. Kyle's tone held that dangerous edge.

Yet it held something else, too, a strained quality that told Longarm Kyle was struggling to stay on his feet. Millie had said he was wounded. He must have heard them coming and managed to hide himself long enough to get the drop on whoever Millie came back with.

"Take it easy," Longarm said, keeping his own voice calm and steady. "From the looks of things, you gave me a hand just now. I ain't looking for trouble with you."

"Yeah, well, I'm looking for something," said Kyle. "I'm looking for answers. Drop that gun and turn around, Parker."

Longarm shook his head slowly. "I'll turn around, but I'm not dropping the gun so you can shoot me down. And if you pull the trigger, you better make sure you kill me with your first shot, otherwise I'll put at least one more bullet in you, too."

Raggedly, Millie said, "For God's sake, Salado, stop it!

139

You're hurt. You're going to bleed to death if you don't get help."

"Shut up, Millie," he snarled. "I'll count to three, Parker . . . one . . . two . . ."

Then there was a groan and a thump, and Millie cried, "Salado!"

Longarm turned around, not hurrying, and saw that Kyle had passed out, just as he suspected might happen if he stalled long enough. The left shoulder of the young man's coat and shirt were stained dark with blood. He lay motionless on the ground underneath the trees. A revolver lay next to his right hand where it had fallen. Longarm kicked it out of reach first, then holstered the Colt and knelt beside the unconscious man.

"Don't you hurt him, damn you."

Longarm glanced over his shoulder and saw that Millie had produced a gun, too, a small pocket pistol that would be deadly enough at this range if she knew how to use it, and from the hard look in her green eyes, she did.

"Take it easy," he told her. "You don't need that gun. I'm not going to hurt your husband."

Working with an expertise that was eloquent testimony to the number of bullet wounds he had patched up in the past, he peeled back Kyle's coat and shirt to reveal the injured shoulder. The bloody, black-rimmed bullethole was low enough so that Longarm thought there was a chance the slug had missed the bone. If that were the case, then this was a messy, painful, but ultimately not life-threatening injury. He said as much.

"You mean you think he'll be all right?" asked Millie anxiously.

"Well, if he doesn't lose too much blood, and that bullethole doesn't fester, he ought to live," Longarm assured her. "You wouldn't happen to have a bottle of whiskey on you, would you?"

She shook her head. "You need a drink at a time like this?"

"If you had some whiskey, I'd pour it on that wound," explained Longarm. "Since you don't, the best thing to do is to get him back to town as fast as we can so the doctor there can tend to him."

"All right. The buggy's parked out there on the road. I'll go get it—"

"Hold on. You're liable to bog down in the mud if you try to drive over here. I'll carry him out of these trees."

Millie stared at him. "You'd do that, you'd help him, after he pointed a gun at you?"

"Well, I'll admit I don't cotton much to having guns pointed at me," said Longarm. "But that don't mean I'd leave a fella to bleed to death."

"Thank you, Mr. Parker."

Longarm slipped his arms under Kyle's body and straightened to his feet with a grunt of effort. The young man was slender, but his dead weight was still quite a burden. Longarm carried him out of the grove of pecan trees and across the field toward the buggy that Millie pointed out. Longarm hadn't noticed the vehicle before, since he'd been a mite occupied with all the lead flying around.

"Can you handle that team?" he asked Millie when he had carefully placed Kyle on the buggy seat.

"I sure can. Are you going to ride back into Buffalo Flat with us?"

"I'll catch up to you," Longarm told her. "I've got to get the lady who's with me."

"Lady? What lady?"

"You just get your husband on to town and don't worry about that."

She nodded and flapped the reins to get the horses moving. Longarm swung back up onto the buckskin and rode around the trees to the bluff. Karen stepped out into the

141

open when she saw him coming. She held the rifle with both hands, slanted across her body.

"What happened?" she asked as Longarm rode up. "I heard the shooting stop, but you didn't come back."

"Some folks gave us a hand. They ran off the bush-whacker, but one of them stopped some lead. I had to help him."

"Who was it?" asked Karen.

"A couple named Kyle. I saw 'em in town last night and again this morning, but I don't reckon you know them . . . unless Charles Stroud mentioned them to you. They came to the bank this morning to talk a little business."

She shook her head blankly. "I don't know what you're talking about."

"Well, it don't matter now. We'll have to double up to get back to town, but this buckskin's strong enough to carry both of us, I reckon."

She handed the rifle up to him and he replaced it in the saddle sheath. Then he gave her a stirrup, grasped her wrist, and pulled her up onto the horse behind him. She straddled the buckskin's back just behind the saddle and put her arms around Longarm's waist to hang on.

"This is most . . . undignified," she said somewhat breathlessly.

"Better than walking," said Longarm as he urged the horse into an easy-gaited trot.

The rain had finally come to a stop. In fact, gaps were beginning to show in the clouds, allowing a little late after-noon sunlight to show through. Longarm and Karen caught up to the other buggy in a few minutes. Despite the urgency that Millie must be feeling, she couldn't drive too quickly on the muddy road. As they came up alongside the vehicle, Longarm looked in and saw that Kyle was still uncon-scious. Millie looked over at him, then looked again when she saw Karen riding behind Longarm with her skirts hiked up and her black boots and stockings visible.

Longarm figured he might as well introduce them. Raising his voice a little so that he could be heard over the hoofbeats of the buggy team and the buckskin, he said, "Karen Wilkes, this is Millie Kyle. Millie, Karen." No point in being too formal, he thought, since he had kissed both of these gals today. Of course, he'd done more than that with Karen . . .

"Hello," Karen said coolly, and Millie just nodded. Both of them demonstrated the reserve that beautiful women usually exhibited on first meeting others of their kind.

"How about telling me what happened back there?" Longarm suggested to Millie. "How did you and your husband get mixed up in that ambush?"

She hesitated, as if weighing how stubborn she wanted to be about answering questions, then said, "We were on our way back to Buffalo Flat from the Circle F, as you've probably figured out. We would have left the ranch sooner, but Mr. Farrell said there was a storm coming and said we ought to wait it out."

"I wish I'd had someone to warn me," said Karen.

Millie ignored the interruption. "We heard shooting, and Salado wanted to find out what was going on." She had stopped even trying not to refer to him by that name, Longarm noticed. "We could tell there was a man in the trees shooting at somebody over by that bluff—"

"That was us," Longarm put in.

Millie nodded. "I know that now. Salado got behind the man and told him to drop his gun, but instead he turned around and shot Salado. I started shooting at him, and Salado was still in the fight, too, even though he was wounded, so the man cut and ran."

"Did you see who he was?" asked Longarm. That was probably the most important question.

Millie shook her head. "No, he had his hat pulled down over his face, and it all happened so fast . . . I just never got a good look at him."

143

"Well, you sure did us a favor by spooking him. I reckon I owe you."

Millie took a deep breath and said, "Then tell me what you know about the money."

"What money?" asked Karen.

Longarm's eyes narrowed as he looked at Millie. The pretty redhead had put her cards on the table. Maybe it was time for Longarm to do the same . . . at least to a certain extent.

"Maybe it *would* be best if we stopped tripping over each other," he said. "We're all after the loot from the Cottonwood Station holdup, right?"

"What loot?" asked Karen.

"That's right," Millie said with a nod. "I heard about it from an old man up in Kansas, who said he was in on the robbery. He claimed the man behind it double-crossed his partners and kept all the money for himself, but he had tracked the man down and intended to reclaim his share of the loot. From what he said, Salado and I figured somebody in Buffalo Flat has the money. How do *you* know about it?"

"My story ain't all that different," said Longarm. "I trailed another old outlaw down here, a fella called Jasper Gammon. I had a pretty good idea he had something to do with that holdup. Never mind how I came by that idea, because it don't matter. What's important is that a couple of hardcases were waiting to ambush Gammon before he got to Buffalo Flat. I think Blaze Harker found out somehow that he was coming."

"Who's Blaze Harker?" asked Karen, having given up on being told about the money.

"The third man in the Cottonwood Station holdup. The one who double-crossed Gammon and . . ." Longarm looked at Millie. "What was the name of the fella up in Kansas?"

"Claude Farley," she said. "Don't worry about him. He's dead, too."

"You killed him?" asked Longarm, a cold edge coming into his voice.

"No, he died on his own. His heart gave out."

Millie blushed some as she said it, and Longarm suddenly wondered what old Claude Farley had been doing when his heart stopped. It was obvious that Millie and Salado weren't what they had claimed to be. It was possible they weren't even married.

He put that aside for the moment and tried to sort out all the new information he had just been told. "So if Farley found out that Blaze Harker was in Buffalo Flat, he could have written to his old partner Jasper Gammon and told him about it, too. They could have planned to meet down here."

"That sounds reasonable enough to me," Millie agreed. "But if this man Harker hired gunmen to ambush them and stop them from getting to Buffalo Flat, how did he know they were coming?"

Longarm shook his head. "I don't know, unless Farley was a big enough fool to get in touch with Harker, too. Maybe he figured that Harker would just pay them off in order to keep his real identity a secret."

"Maybe," Millie said. "But like you said, it was a foolish thing to do."

Longarm smiled. "Most outlaws don't get into that line of work because they're smart."

Karen said, "I don't have the slightest idea what you two are talking about, but I think it's going to start raining again."

Longarm glanced up at the sky and saw that she was right. The gaps in the clouds had closed up again, and now the gloom was growing thick. The wind blew harder. The respite from the storm had been only temporary.

"We're not far from town now," he said. "Maybe we can get there before it gets too bad."

This time that hope bore more fruit. It was raining by the time they reached Buffalo Flat, but not the drenching downpour that had battered the land earlier in the day.

Longarm urged the buckskin ahead of the buggy, leading the way to Dr. Maxwell's office. As they got there, Karen said, "Custis, from what you were saying to that woman, I get the idea that you're much more than what you appear to be."

"I'm just a fella trying to sort everything out," he said as he reined in.

"And track down a fortune in stolen money."

He shrugged. "I wouldn't mind finding it. And it would sure be a help if you could see your way clear not to talk about any of this to anybody."

"Because you don't know who this Blaze Harker really is. He might be pretending to be anybody in Buffalo Flat. That's why you've been talking to so many people and asking so many questions." She paused. "Almost like a lawman."

"You said that, not me."

With his help, she slid down from the back of the horse and then looked up at him. "You don't have to worry, Custis. I won't say anything."

He nodded and let his hand cup her chin for a moment. "I'm much obliged."

The buggy pulled up then, before they could say or do anything else. Longarm dismounted and went over to the vehicle to help Millie get Salado down from the seat. The wounded man was partially conscious by now, but he couldn't walk or hold himself up. That took the efforts of both Longarm and Millie.

When Longarm glanced around as they stepped up onto the porch of the doctor's office, he saw that Karen was gone.

Maxwell had his living quarters behind the office. The lights were on back there. Longarm stood there holding up Salado while Millie pounded on the door and called out. A few moments later, the door opened and the doctor demanded irritably, "What's all the banging and caterwauling out here?"

"Got a wounded man, Doc," said Longarm.

"Oh." Maxwell's attitude changed instantly. "Bring him in, then, and be quick about it. No patient has ever died yet on my front porch, and I'd like to keep it that way."

Longarm and Millie took Salado into the examining room and got him up on the table. Maxwell moved in then and went to work with practiced efficiency, cleaning the wound and checking Salado's back for an exit wound. Finding none, he announced, "The bullet's still in there. It'll have to come out. Let me give this young man a little laudanum."

Longarm admired the way Maxwell did his job without asking a lot of questions about how Salado had come to be wounded. Dealing with the injury was the main thing; finding out what had happened could wait until later.

Using a probe and forceps, Maxwell quickly located and extracted the slug. He dropped the bloody, misshapen lump of lead into a basin. Longarm looked at it for a long moment.

Maxwell noted his interest and grunted. "Second bullet I've dug out of somebody today," the doctor commented. "At least this victim's still alive."

"You're talking about that bushwhacker who was brought in from the Circle F this morning?"

Maxwell nodded as he cleaned the wound in Salado's shoulder again. "That's right. That man was shot from the front, though, rather than the back."

"What did you do with the bullet?" asked Longarm idly.

"Marshal Gibbs has it."

The medico fell silent again as he wound bandages

147

around Salado's shoulder and tied them tightly in place. He looked over at the wan, worried Millie and asked, "Is this man your husband?"

"Yes," she said. "Yes, he is."

"Well, I'm pretty sure he'll be all right, but he'll need to stay here for a few days. He'll hurt bad enough tomorrow that he won't want to go anywhere anyway."

Millie nodded. "All right. Whatever you think is best, Doc."

Maxwell looked at Longarm. "Help me get him into a bed, and then you folks can go on about your business."

"Can I . . . can I stay here with him?" asked Millie.

"Well . . . it's not really necessary, but I don't suppose there's any harm in it. You'll have to sleep in a chair, though."

"That's all right." She stood by the examining table and rested a hand on Salado's uninjured shoulder. "I don't mind."

A few minutes later, after they had gotten Salado settled into a bed in the doctor's front room, Longarm and Millie stepped out onto the porch for a moment.

"When Salado wakes up, he's not going to be happy that I told you about why we're here," said Millie.

Longarm shrugged. "Sometimes it's better to join forces than to keep working at cross-purposes."

"I'm not sure I can trust you, even though we've helped each other."

"I reckon that's a risk we all have to take," Longarm pointed out.

Millie nodded. "Yes, I guess you're right. I need to get back inside with Salado. You'll let us know if you find out anything?"

"Sure," said Longarm. Millie looked like she didn't really believe him, but she smiled faintly and nodded. Then she turned and went back into the building.

Longarm drew a deep breath. The rain was falling heavier now that night had descended on Buffalo Flat. It distorted the glow of lighted windows in the buildings along the street. Longarm reached for a cheroot, only to remember that they had all gotten soaked earlier in the day, along with everything else. He'd have to pick up some more. Grimacing in disappointment, he started walking toward the marshal's office. He wanted to have a talk with Gibbs.

He was passing the dark mouth of an alley when a man came running out of it, plowed smack-dab into him, and knocked both of them sprawling in the mud.

Chapter 17

"What the hell!"

The exclamation was uttered in a familiar voice. Longarm pushed himself up into a sitting position and looked over to see the local banker, Charles Stroud, also sitting in the mud. Stroud wore a yellow slicker, and a derby hat had fallen off his head. The rain slicked down his hair. He pushed it back, wiping a dark smudge off his forehead at the same time, and clapped his hat back on, mud and all.

"You're in an almighty big hurry," Longarm said as he climbed to his feet and started trying to wipe some of the mud off his clothes. The rain helped a little, washing away the stuff in places. He glanced over into the alley and saw the horse Stroud had been leading.

"I'm looking for Karen . . . Miss Wilkes," said Stroud as he got up out of the mud, too. His voice held a thin edge of panic. "She left town this afternoon to take a drive, and she never came back."

"Is that all that's got you worried?"

"All?" echoed Stroud. "She's missing! Isn't that enough?"

"How long ago did you check her house?"

"About half an hour ago, I guess."

151

He must have just missed her, thought Longarm. "I'd go by there again, if I was you. I happen to know that's about the time she got back to town."

Stroud stared at him in confusion. "How would you know about that, Mr. Parker?" He reached up and brushed at his forehead again distractedly.

"I was on my way back from the Circle F and ran into Miss Wilkes just before the storm started this afternoon. It got so bad that a tree nearly fell on us when it blew down, so we found a place to wait it out, then came on into town a little while ago."

"Is that so?" asked Stroud coldly. "Where did you wait?"

"Under a big, overhanging limestone bluff."

The banker nodded. "I know the place." He looked down at the slicker and brushed more mud off it. "Well, I suppose there's no need for me to go galloping around the countryside looking for her, then. I'll take my horse back to the livery and clean up a little before I go over to her house. Sorry about running into you."

"Just an accident," shrugged Longarm. He stepped closer to Stroud's horse. "I can give you a hand if you want. I got to put my buckskin up, so I could take your horse, too."

"No, that's all right. Thanks anyway." Stroud took the reins and turned the horse around, then trudged back along the alley.

Longarm frowned in thought as he watched the banker vanish into the rain. He wasn't sure what Karen was going to tell Stroud about the events of the afternoon. He had asked her not to say anything about the ambush, but how was she going to explain the fact that her buggy was still out at the base of that bluff, along with the dead horses?

Slowly, Longarm shook his head. There was nothing he could do about that now. He wanted to go back to the hotel, dry off, and put on some clean clothes, but he had to pay a visit to Marshal Gibbs' office, too, and since he was already wet he thought he might as well go ahead and do that, rather than coming back out once he had changed.

A light glowed in the window of the marshal's office. Longarm went in without knocking and found Hannibal Gibbs sitting at the desk, looking at some papers spread out in front of him. Most of them were wanted posters, but there was a telegraph flimsy there, too. As Longarm closed the door, Gibbs looked up at him and said in his high-pitched voice, "Parker. I was just thinkin' about comin' to look for you."

"I reckon I saved you some trouble, then," said Longarm.

"Yeah." Gibbs grinned. "Wet and muddy like that, you look like somethin' the cat dragged in."

"I feel about like that, too." Longarm took off his hat and hung it on a nail beside the door.

"If you're gonna sit down, take that wooden chair," said Gibbs. "I don't want you gettin' the sofa muddy."

Longarm glanced at the old, sagging sofa and debated whether or not a little mud would hurt it, but he went along with the marshal's request. He picked up a ladder-backed wooden chair and swung it around so he could straddle it. As he sat down, he asked, "You wouldn't happen to have a cheroot, would you?"

"Nope. Sorry." Gibbs picked up the telegram from his desk. "I've got this, though . . . Marshal."

Longarm stiffened, surprise flooding through him.

Gibbs's grin widened as he went on, "Custis Long, ain't it? I thought you looked a mite familiar when I first saw you, but I didn't place you until late this afternoon. Then it came to me. I saw you up in Denver, three, maybe four years ago, when I was payin' a visit to Billy Vail. Billy didn't introduce us, but he told me later you were one of his deputies."

"You know Billy Vail?" asked Longarm.

"We used to ride together in the Rangers, a long time

back. Once I remembered who you were, I sent him a wire and asked him why you were in my town." Gibbs's voice hardened a little. "You should've told me who you were, Long. That would've been the proper thing to do."

Longarm nodded curtly. "I know it, and I meant no offense, Marshal. But I was working undercover when I rode in, and I wanted to see what I could turn up before I laid my cards on the table."

Gibbs grunted and said, "I reckon I can understand that. But let's not have any more secrets between us, all right?"

"Sure," agreed Longarm. "Did Billy tell you why I'm here?"

One of the local lawman's blunt fingers tapped the telegram. "He said you're on the trail of the loot from the Cottonwood Station holdup. That you've got reason to believe somebody here in Buffalo Flat may have been in on it."

"Blaze Harker," Longarm said with a nod. "Best I can put it together, he masterminded the whole deal and pulled the robbery with a couple of partners named Jasper Gammon and Claude Farley."

"Gammon," repeated Gibbs. "The old-timer who got ambushed yesterday."

Longarm nodded again. "That's right. He's dead, and so is Farley. He died up in Kansas." Longarm didn't say anything about the connection Millie and Salado had with Farley. He had promised to lay his cards on the table with Gibbs, but there was no need to bring those two into it, at least not yet. He didn't know if they would play square with him, but he was willing to give them the benefit of the doubt for now.

Anyway, they might be out of it, because a picture was starting to form in his mind. Several things he had seen today linked together, he realized, and if he could find a few more pieces of the puzzle to bridge the remaining gaps . . .

"So this Blaze Harker owlhoot is the only one left,"

Gibbs was saying. "And you think he's here in Buffalo Flat, livin' under another name?"

"I think this is where he came after the holdup," said Longarm. "He brought the loot here and assumed another identity, maybe even one he had already set up."

"And he's been here ever since?"

Longarm thought about that. "More than likely. He's probably still here, although I can't be sure about that just yet."

Gibbs leaned forward and asked sharply, "You know where he is?"

"Maybe."

Gibbs slapped a hand on the desk. "Damn it, Long, you said you was gonna come clean with me!"

"And I will," promised Longarm, "as soon as I check on a few more things. You can help me with that."

Gibbs was angry at Longarm's evasiveness, but he grudgingly asked, "What do you want from me?"

"Doc Maxwell said he gave you the bullet he dug out of the bushwhacker who was brought in from the Circle F today."

Gibbs frowned in puzzlement. "Yeah. Was that the same fella who got away yesterday?"

Longarm nodded and said, "That's right. They were hired to watch the trails into town and given Jasper Gammon's description. It was their job to keep him from reaching Buffalo Flat alive. They succeeded in that, even though it cost one of them his life. Then today, the other one was sent after me."

"By Blaze Harker!" exclaimed Gibbs. "Damn it, it's startin' to make sense now."

"Let me take a look at that bullet, and maybe it'll make even more sense."

Gibbs gave a little shake of his head. "Wait just a dog-goned minute. It was a couple of Circle F punchers who brought in that bushwhacker's body, and they said that Beth Ferrell was the one who shot him."

"Let's see the bullet," Longarm said again.

Gibbs opened the desk drawer and took out a flattened slug. He placed it on the desk between him and Longarm, and both of them looked closely at it. A smile of satisfaction spread slowly across Longarm's weary features.

"Damn it!" burst out Gibbs. "What the hell's so important about this bullet?"

"It's a forty-four-forty," said Longarm. "A rifle bullet, more than likely. Beth Ferrell was carrying a thirty-eight revolver."

"Then Beth . . ." Gibbs struggled with it for a second. "Beth didn't shoot that bushwhacker."

"She shot *at* him, right enough. But she didn't mean to hit him, and she was mighty surprised when he turned up dead. That's because she *didn't* hit him." Quickly, Longarm explained how the bushwhacker had ambushed him and how Beth had flushed the man out of hiding on the wooded hill. "When the fella ran, somebody else took a long-range shot and put that bullet in his back. He lived long enough to run into me, but not long enough to talk. I'd say that was just what the killer intended. He didn't want that hired gun being able to answer any questions."

Gibbs nodded. "Yeah, I reckon that makes sense. And it all comes back to Harker. He's got to be behind everything. He's the one who killed that bushwhacker."

Longarm didn't address that issue. Instead he pointed to the spent slug and said, "The fella who fired that has had a busy day. He tried later to kill me again."

"The hell you say! Why didn't he just take a shot at you earlier, instead of gunnin' down that fella he hired?"

"I reckon he didn't have a clear shot at me from where he was," mused Longarm. "So he just did what he could at the moment. He tried to make up for it later on, though."

156

Gibbs rubbed his heavy jaw. "So what are you gonna do now? You plan to arrest Blaze Harker?"

"Not just yet." *And likely not ever*, he added to himself. "There's still the matter of that stolen money."

"Get Harker behind bars and he'll talk!" Gibbs said with a snort.

Longarm shook his head. "No, Harker won't tell us where he hid the money. But I've got an idea about that I want to check out."

"And you don't plan on tellin' me what it is, either, do you?"

"Sorry, Marshal. I'm not trying to be mysterious. I'm just still not sure about some things, and I want to get all the pieces put together before I make a move against the man I'm after."

Gibbs frowned. "Well . . . I don't much like it. But I'd trust Billy Vail with my life—hell, I did just that, more'n once back in the old days—and if he trusts you I reckon that's good enough for me. But you'll let me know if you need my help, won't you?"

"You can count on that, Marshal," Longarm assured him. He stood up and retrieved his hat from the nail. "Where can I find you if I need you?" asked Gibbs.

"I've got to see to my horse, and then I'm heading for the hotel. It's been a mighty long day."

Gibbs nodded. "All right. Try not to get shot at."

"I always try," said Longarm with a grin. "It's just that other folks don't always cooperate."

He left the office and walked outside, his eyes searching the rainy night for any sign of trouble. It was entirely possible that the man he was after would make another attempt on his life. He would need eyes in the back of his head. Luckily, his long, eventful career as a lawman had honed his instincts until they were about as sharp as humanly possible.

He got the buckskin from the hitch rack in front of the doctor's office and led the horse down the street to the livery stable. "Sorry you had to stand out in the rain for so long, old son," murmured Longarm.

Ed Schmitt wasn't at the livery stable, having gone home for the night. An elderly hostler was there instead, and the old-timer complained when Longarm brought in the buckskin.

"This ain't a night fittin' for anybody to be out and about," he said querulously as Longarm began to unsaddle the horse. "All this damp weather makes my rheumatism act up somethin' fierce."

"Not a very busy night, eh?" asked Longarm as he rubbed down the buckskin.

"Hell, no. You're the only one who ain't got sense enough to come in outta the rain."

Longarm poured some feed from a bucket into the trough in the buckskin's stall and inclined his head toward the barn across the street. "What about the other place? They doing any business?"

"One other dumb son of a bitch brought a hoss in about twenty minutes ago. That's been the only comin's and goin's on this end o' town tonight."

"Well, sorry I bothered you," said Longarm mildly, not responding to the implied insult the old man had given him. "I shouldn't need my horse again tonight."

The elderly hostler snorted in disgust. "I should hope not!"

Longarm walked back down the street to the hotel. The clerk at the desk gave him the skunk eye as Longarm walked dripping and muddy through the lobby. The big lawman got his key and went on up to his room, not really caring what anybody else thought. It had been a long, tiring day, and he had a lot to think about. He was pretty sure now that he had everything figured out, but he wanted to go over it in his head one more time, maybe even sleep on it before he did anything else. He didn't think his quarry was going to leave town, at least not right away. The man had too much invested in his masquerade.

Longarm wasn't going to get to ponder things just yet, though. When he reached his room, he glanced down instinctively and suddenly stiffened as he saw that the matchstick he had wedged between the door and the jamb when he left the room that morning was gone.

Somebody had been in there.

Somebody might still be in there, waiting to kill him.

Chapter 18

He kept walking along the corridor with barely a hitch in his stride, hoping that if a would-be killer was lurking inside the room that he wouldn't have noticed the momentary hesitation in Longarm's footsteps. Longarm wanted the son of a bitch to think that he was some other guest of the hotel, on his way to a different room.

When he was two doors past the door to his own room, he stopped and reached down to pull his boots off. It wasn't an easy chore since his socks were wet, but he managed. Then, quietly, he catfooted back to his own door, carrying the boots.

He put them down when he got there, then slipped his gun out of its holster and held the key in his other hand. For a moment he listened intently but didn't hear any sounds coming from inside the room. It was entirely possible that he was being too cautious . . . but when you really came right down to it, there was no such thing in his line of work. There was only cautious enough—and dead.

He jammed the key into the lock, twisted it, flung the door open, and went into the room in a rolling dive, all in the space of a heartbeat.

A sharp cry of surprise came from the direction of the

bed as he wound up in a crouch, his Colt pointing in that direction. His finger was taut on the trigger, but he held off from squeezing it. The lamp on the table was burning, so he had a good look at the intruder.

Millie Kyle sat there with her back propped against the headboard, her green eyes wide with surprise and fear as she stared down the barrel of the gun. Longarm couldn't see all of her because the sheet was over the lower half of her body, but she was nude from the waist up, at least. Her small but firm breasts, crowned with pink nipples, had a scattering of freckles across them. Her long red hair was loose and hung around her shoulders. She was damned cute.

But what the hell was she doing in his bed?

"You don't have to shoot me, Mr. Parker," she said, her voice trembling a little. "I'm not here to cause trouble for you."

Longarm straightened. He didn't holster the Colt just yet, not until he had taken a look around the room and seen that no one else was lurking in here. He didn't think Salado was in any shape to be trying an ambush, not with that wounded shoulder of his, but you never could tell about such things.

Millie was alone, though, and after a moment Longarm slipped the revolver back into the cross-draw rig. He reached out into the hall, picked up his boots, and closed the door. "What are you doing here?" he asked bluntly.

Now that she knew he wasn't going to shoot her, Millie relaxed a little. She made no attempt to draw the sheet up and cover her bare breasts.

"Salado sent me," she said.

Longarm frowned. "To do what, exactly?"

Millie's creamy skin flushed. "To talk to you. I have to admit, he didn't say anything about doing it like . . . this. That was my idea."

Longarm grunted and dropped his hat on a chair. "Why

162

don't you tell me about it? The talking to part, that is, not the rest of it."

She took a deep breath, which didn't do anything to lessen the distraction her current state of nudity was causing. "All right. After a while, he woke up from that laudanum the doc gave him, and he wanted to know where he was and what had happened. I told him all about it, including the fact that you and I talked about how we're all looking for the loot from Cottonwood Station. He was upset about that, just like I figured he would be. But when I told him we might come closer to finding it by working with you, rather than against you, he calmed down and understood."

"Because he figured the two of you could always double-cross me and kill me once we got our hands on the loot," Longarm said dryly.

"I wouldn't know about that. I know *I* never thought that." She paused and then went on, "In my line of work, a girl gets to where she can tell a lot about a man in a hurry. I think you're an honest man, Mr. Parker. If you make a deal with somebody, you'll hold up your end of the bargain."

"And what line of work are you in?" he asked, even though he figured he already knew the answer.

She blushed again. "I'm a whore. I *was* a whore. I don't reckon I am anymore, at least not now. And Salado's not a businessman, like he's been telling everybody. He's a gambler. Just saloon trash like me, I guess you could say. And we're not married, either." She smiled. "There. I've told you the truth. And it feels pretty good. I'm not really cut out for pretending to be somebody I'm not."

Longarm nodded. "I appreciate that. But it still doesn't explain why you're here, or how you knew this was my room."

"Salado wanted me to get your word that you'll play square with us. That's all. He knew this was your room because he got a look at the register without the clerk knowing about it, before we went out to the Circle F. The lock wasn't tricky enough to keep me out. As for the rest of it . . ." She looked down at her state of undress. "I figured maybe we ought to seal the bargain."

Longarm started to unbutton his shirt.

Millie smiled in satisfaction.

But then he said, "I'm cold and wet and worn-out, Millie. I want to clean up, dry off, and get some sleep. That's all. You probably ought to get your clothes on and go back over to the doc's place. Tell Salado I promised not to double-cross the two of you."

She stared at him in surprise. "You don't want me?" Her eyes dropped to the growing bulge at his groin. "I know you do. I can see that you do."

"Hell, I'm human," he growled. "Most fellas are gonna stand up and take notice any time they find a pretty young redhead in their bed. But rompin' is pretty low down on my list of priorities right now."

She pushed the sheet back, swung her long, creamy legs out of bed, and stood up. Yep, thought Longarm, she was nude from the waist down, too. The large bush of bright red hair at the juncture of her thighs drew his eye. He couldn't help it.

She moved closer to him. His shirt was open now, and she rested her hands on his muscular, hairy chest. "Let me help you clean up, at least," she murmured. "There's a basin and a cloth on the table. I'm good at things like that. There's a reason they call it a whore's bath, you know."

The nearness of her aroused Longarm even more. "You don't have to do anything," he told her in a low voice.

"I know that. I want to."

He was too tired to argue with her. He stood there and let her strip his clothes off him, one piece at a time, until he was nude. Then she fetched the cloth and the basin of water and washed him all over. The coolness of the room made goosebumps stand up on his skin until he got used to it.

Millie finished by kneeling in front of him and wrapping the wet cloth around his erect shaft. She pumped it up and down. Longarm said, "I don't recall getting that in the mud today."

"Hush," she said softly. Then she dropped the cloth, leaned forward, and took the head of his organ in her mouth.

Longarm closed his eyes and let her demonstrate her skills on him. She was good at what she was doing, every bit as good as Karen Wilkes had been earlier in the day. Now if he could just get Beth Ferrell in his bed before the night was over, he would have made a clean sweep of the good-looking gals he had run into on this job, and in mighty short order, too.

But that wasn't going to happen. Beth was out on the Circle F. Her part in this was over, and he didn't really expect to see her again. If she had any sense, he thought, she would go ahead and marry Bob Teague and settle down. Teague seemed like a good enough fella, and he was in love with her, that was for sure. They could get hitched and raise a passel of kids and run that ranch together, and it would be a mighty fine life for the two of them.

Thinking about that kept his mind off the excitement that was building up inside him, at least for a little while. But then Millie lifted her head and said, "Lay down on the bed. I know you're tired, Mr. Parker, so I'll do all the work."

"Custis," he said. "Call me Custis . . ."

She lived up to her word. He stretched out on his back, with his long, thick erection jutting up proudly from his groin, and all he had to do was lie there and enjoy it as she played with it and licked it and sucked it some more. Then she straddled him, grasped the thick pole, and guided it to her opening as she sank down slowly onto it, sheathing him inside her. She let out a little gasp when she hit bottom. Then she sat there for a moment, trembling a little from the sheer pleasure of being filled so completely.

Longarm reached up and took her breasts in his hands, strumming the erect nipples with his thumbs. That made Millie's hips start pumping. She rode him slowly at first, but then the pace of her movements increased. She began to rotate her hips, alternating with the straight-ahead thrusts. Longarm had slept with many professional gals in the past. They were always skilled at what they did, but they had a certain reserve, a barrier they had learned to put up between themselves and the men they took into their bodies. That barrier usually dissolved when Longarm made love to them, and he began to see that happening now with Millie. Her breath came faster and her eyes grew heavy-lidded. She made an involuntary noise deep in her throat. Her thrusts became stronger, more urgent. She rode him now like it meant something, and it did.

Suddenly she sprawled forward on his chest and kissed him. He tangled a hand in her long red hair and speared his tongue into her mouth. Her hips bounced wildly as she galloped toward the finish line.

Millie wasn't the only one caught up in the moment. Longarm's fatigue had fallen away from him, and he matched her with equally enthusiastic thrusts of his own, burying his shaft as deeply inside her as it would go and then pulling out part of the way only to drive back into her. It was a timeless, universal coupling, a natural rhythm that washed away everything else. Longarm grabbed her hips and pistoned in and out of her.

Their culmination exploded over both of them at the same time, rippling through them in shudders and spasms. Longarm's seed filled her. She cried out against his mouth and flooded him with her own juices. The exquisite sensation seemed to last forever. When it was finally over she slumped against him, as limp as if every bone in her body had suddenly turned to jelly. He felt pretty much the same way himself.

Longarm held her for a moment while he caught his

breath. He stroked her hair and moved his hand on down her back to the graceful curve of her hips. Millie rested her face against his shoulder.

When she could speak again, she said, "I swear, Custis, that wasn't like . . . wasn't like what I usually do . . . I never expected . . ."

"I know," Longarm told her quietly. "You don't have to say anything else."

She snuggled against him and he held her some more, and he began to worry that they might go to sleep like that. He was about to tell her that she ought to get up, put her clothes on, and go back to the doctor's house. He would even offer to walk her over there.

That was when an urgent knock suddenly sounded on the door.

Millie gasped and lifted her head. "Who—" she whispered.

Longarm touched her lips with a fingertip. He rolled her off him, sat up, and reached for the shell belt that he had coiled and placed on the table next to the bed, so that the butt of the Colt was in easy reach. As he closed his fingers around the walnut grips, the knock came again. "Mr. Parker?" a female voice said. "Custis, are you in there?"

Longarm knew that voice. It belonged to Karen Wilkes.

"Who's *that*?" asked Millie in a whisper. Scorn dripped from her voice. Her claws were coming out in an instinctive female reaction, thought Longarm.

"Take it easy," he told her. "It's just that lady I was with earlier today when we got bushwhacked."

"She sounds mighty friendly with you."

Longarm laid the gun on the table and reached for his pants. He called through the door, "Just a minute." As he pulled his trousers up, he added quietly to Millie, "You can stay right there."

"Thank you," she said coldly.

Longarm ignored her tone and went to the door, the gun

in his hand again just in case. He opened the door, but only a few inches. As far as he could tell, Karen Wilkes was alone in the hallway, with a worried, agitated expression on her face.

"Oh, Custis, I'm glad you're here," she said. "I have to talk to you."

Longarm nodded. "Go ahead. What's wrong?"

Karen hesitated and then asked, "Can I come in?"

"Might be better if you didn't."

"Oh." Realization dawned in her blue eyes. "Oh! You're not alone, are you?"

Now she was mad at him, he thought as he made an effort to unclench his jaw. "Just tell me what's wrong."

"All right," she said, her tone as chilly as Millie's had been a minute earlier. "It's Charles."

"Stroud? What about him?"

Karen's anger dissipated as a somewhat embarrassed look came over her face. "I'm afraid I lied to you this afternoon, Custis," she said. "I wasn't just taking a drive when that storm came along. I was out there for a reason. I was following Charles."

Longarm nodded. He wasn't completely surprised by what Karen had just told him. "You saw him ride out, and you wondered where he was going."

"That's right. Charles has a horse that he keeps at Jonas's Livery, but he hardly ever uses it. I don't know why I . . . I felt like I had to follow him, but I was curious. And then . . . I guess I'm not very good at trailing somebody, because I lost sight of him and never saw him again. I drove around for a while, hoping I'd find him, but when I didn't I decided I'd better come back to town. That was when you came along, and then that storm blew in, and that man started shooting at us . . ." Her voice trailed off and she shuddered, hugging herself.

"It's all right," Longarm told her. "That's all over now. What brings you here tonight?"

168

"I saw Charles a little while ago, going into the bank. He seemed . . . upset." She raised her chin. "I told you the truth this afternoon, Custis, about not wanting to marry Charles. But I *am* fond of him, and I think he must be in some sort of trouble. I think you have something to do with it, too."

"What gives you that idea?" asked Longarm.

"Well . . . you ride into Buffalo Flat, and suddenly things start happening. You've only been here about twenty-four hours, and three men have been killed, and people keep shooting at you, and . . . and now Charles is acting strange, driving a wagon into the alley beside the bank—"

Longarm's hand shot out and gripped her arm. "A wagon, you say?"

Karen looked surprised by the vehemence of his reaction. She jerked her head in a nod and said, "Yes. I don't know what's going on, Custis, but I thought maybe you could tell me."

There was no time for that, thought Longarm. All hell was about to bust loose, and if he didn't hurry he was going to miss it. He opened the door wider and pulled a startled Karen into the room. Behind him in the bed, Millie let out a gasp. Longarm glanced over his shoulder and saw that at least she had pulled the sheet up so that she was covered.

"I knew you had a woman in here with you!" said Karen. "I'm not surprised that it's this redheaded tramp."

"Tramp!" exclaimed Millie. "You got no right—"

"The two of you stay here," Longarm interrupted as he hurriedly pulled on his clothes and stomped his feet down into his boots. He buckled the gunbelt around his waist and reached for his hat.

"Where are you going?" the two of them asked at the same time.

"To see a man about some money," Longarm replied grimly, and then he was gone before they could say anything else.

Chapter 19

Stroud had panicked and was moving faster than Longarm had expected him to. Longarm had figured that he had until morning, at the very least, and really thought that the banker would stay and try to bluff it out. But clearly, Stroud had decided to take off for the tall and uncut while he had the chance, even if it meant abandoning everything he had worked for so long to achieve.

If he succeeded in getting away, he would have plenty of money to make a new start somewhere else, that was for sure.

The rain had stopped again, but the street was muddy as Longarm hurried across it toward the bank. No lights showed inside the building's front windows. Stroud would be working in the back, probably with a hooded lantern. Longarm drew his Colt as he started stealthily along the alley beside the bank.

He heard horses stamping restlessly as he reached the rear corner of the building. Edging an eye around the corner, he saw the dark bulk of the wagon parked there, with four horses hitched to it. The back door of the bank was open, and a faint light spilled from it into the rear alley. As Longarm watched, a shadow crossed that light, and

Charles Stroud came out of the bank, carrying a wooden chest that was evidently pretty heavy. He placed it in the back of the wagon under a canvas cover that was partially thrown back. There were several similar chests already in the wagon.

Stroud straightened and stepped away from the vehicle, but before he could re-enter the bank, Longarm moved around the corner and leveled the Colt. "Hold it right there, Stroud," he said coldly.

Stroud wore the same duster and black hat he had worn earlier in the day when he tried to kill Longarm and Karen. He probably had a gun under that duster, but he stood stiffly still and made no move to reach for it. He turned his head to look along the alley, and his voice was like flint as he said, "Deputy Long. I thought you were just another outlaw trying to horn in, like Gammon and Claude Farley."

"I don't hold with train robbery," said Longarm, "but those fellas had more of a right to that money than you do, old son."

"The hell they did!" Stroud burst out. "They were just hired guns, not really partners. Blaze Harker planned the whole thing. There never would have been a Cottonwood Station holdup if not for him!"

"Well, you're proud of your old man, anyway. I guess that's saying something for you." Longarm paused, then went on inexorably, "But you're still under arrest for murder. You had Gammon killed, and then you gunned down that hardcase today rather than let him fall into my hands. You'll probably swing for that. Hell, if you'd just turned over the money when your father died, you probably wouldn't even have gone to prison."

"But it was mine!" snarled Stroud. "I deserved it. I won't ever give it up."

"Looks like it's a mite late for that. You're under arrest, remember?"

172

Longarm saw a smile stretch slowly across Stroud's face. "I don't think so."

That was an old trick, but a cold feeling in Longarm's gut told him that this time it was genuine. So did Karen's voice as she said from behind him, "Put the gun down, Custis. I'll shoot if I have to."

Longarm didn't move. He kept the Colt trained on Stroud as he said, "That son of a bitch tried to kill you this afternoon, remember?"

"That was before I knew what was going on. Charles and I have . . . reached an understanding, I suppose you could say."

"You mean he offered to share the loot with you," Longarm said flatly. "That's why you came over to the hotel and baited this trap for me."

"That's right. Anyway, Charles was really trying to kill *you*. I really did follow him just to see what he was doing, and I just happened to be in the wrong place at the wrong time. Now I'm in the right place at the right time." Her voice hardened as she said, "Put the gun down."

"I can blow Stroud's head off before you can kill me," said Longarm.

"I didn't say I'd shoot you."

That cold feeling in Longarm's stomach was a block of ice now. He heard a faint moan and knew that Karen had probably just jabbed Millie with that gun barrel. With a sigh, he slowly lowered the Colt and then let it slip from his fingers to the muddy floor of the alley. When he looked around, he saw that Karen had an arm looped around Millie's neck and a small but deadly pistol pressed to the side of her head. Millie's clothes were disheveled. She had probably been forced to get dressed at gunpoint.

Stroud rushed over and scooped up the gun Longarm had dropped. "Good work, Karen," he said.

Then he viciously smashed the butt of the Colt against

Longarm's head and sent the lawman sprawling face down in the mud. Longarm wondered if he would drown in the stuff, and that was the last thought he had before darkness engulfed him.

He woke up, which was a bit of a surprise in itself. Stroud and Karen wouldn't have wanted the sound of a gunshot to rouse the town, but they could have cut his throat. They probably had something else in mind that would be even worse.

That was the case, all right. Longarm pried his eyes open and saw that he was lying on the floor of a small, dim, windowless room. Millie was beside him, evidently unconscious. A trickle of blood leaked from a gash above her ear. Stroud had probably pistol-whipped her, too, thought Longarm as anger surged through him.

He heard voices from somewhere nearby. "You're sure they won't be able to get out?"

"Positive. Once the vault door is closed, there's no way to open it from inside. And I changed the combination on the lock to one that nobody else knows. Long and the girl won't be able to get out, and no one will be able to get in. This is an airtight vault, one of the sturdiest west of the Mississippi. My father paid plenty to have it installed. They'll suffocate long before anybody can get to them."

Longarm seethed at the tone of smug satisfaction he heard in Charles Stroud's voice. Not that Stroud was the bastard's real name. Maybe Charles was, but he'd been born a Harker. Longarm remembered the portrait he had seen of Benjamin Stroud, the founder of this bank. What better way to conceal that white streak in his hair than to shave his head? There was certainly less chance of being discovered that way than there was in dying the streak black, like Charles Stroud did to cover up the trait he had inherited. Dye could run, as it had tonight when Stroud's hair got wet. Longarm had seen that smudge on the banker's forehead and recognized it for what it was, and with that, the rest of the puzzle had finally come together. He had seen the butt of the Winchester sticking up from a saddle scabbard on Stroud's horse, too. A lot of men carried rifles that fired .44-40 cartridges, but the fact that Stroud was one of them convinced Longarm that his theory was correct. When the hostler at Schmitt's livery had told him that someone had brought a horse in to the stable across the street but nobody had taken one out, Longarm had figured that Stroud was on his way back into town when they had collided, rather than leaving. The banker had changed out of his bushwhacking clothes somewhere on the way into Buffalo Flat. It added up to Stroud being guilty as hell.

All of this flashed through Longarm's brain in a heartbeat as he lay there gathering his strength. The fact that he had figured out where the loot from the Cottonwood Station robbery had been hidden all these years wouldn't do him a damned bit of good if Stroud and Karen shut him up in here with Millie to die of suffocation. If the vault was as strong as Stroud claimed, the only way in would be to dynamite the door. By the time the people of Buffalo Flat realized Stroud was missing and got around to doing that, of course, he and Millie would already be dead . . .

Longarm raised his head. He saw the thick, heavy vault door about ten feet from him. The shelves inside the vault were empty. Stroud had already cleaned it out, taking not only the loot from the robbery but also the bank's legitimate deposits. The town would be ruined when Stroud absconded with all the funds.

Now Stroud was saying, "Are you sure you want to go through with this, Karen? You can stand killing them?"

"For that much money?" Karen Wilkes laughed. "I can stand it, Charles. Trust me. I can stand it."

Longarm grimaced. Karen had changed her tune mighty quick-like. All it had taken was a share of a fortune.

Footsteps approached the vault. At the same time, Millie let out a soft groan and started to stir as she regained consciousness. She blinked her eyes and tried to sit up. Longarm reached out to press her back down. They had to take Stroud and Karen by surprise if they were going to have a chance to turn the tables on them . . .

Then suddenly, as Stroud loomed in the doorway of the vault, a door was thrown open somewhere else and a new voice shouted, "Hold it, you bastard! Where's Millie?"

"Salado!" yelped Millie before Longarm could stop her.

Stroud twisted, his hand flashing under the duster, and guns roared in the room just outside the vault.

No point in waiting now, thought Longarm as he lunged up from the floor of the vault. Millie was right behind him.

He was still a little dizzy from being knocked out, but danger cleared away the cobwebs in a hurry. Stroud had vanished, but guns were still going off, so close that the reports were deafening. As Longarm and Millie emerged from the vault, the lawman saw that Stroud and Salado Kyle were firing at each other across the room. Salado was suddenly thrown back against the open door as one of Stroud's shots slammed into his body. Millie screamed and started toward him, but Karen Wilkes got in her way and slashed at her head with a pistol. Millie blocked the blow, grabbed Karen's arm, and slung her around, sending her falling through the open door into the vault. Millie threw her weight against the door to swing it shut.

Karen screamed, a terrified howl that was cut off by the loud clang of the vault door closing.

Meanwhile, Stroud whirled toward Longarm and triggered twice, forcing Longarm to dive headfirst to the floor. The bullets whipped over his head. As he scrambled up again, Stroud leaped over Salado's fallen form and out the door, vanishing into the night. Longarm went after him, pausing only long enough to snatch up the revolver Salado had dropped.

A flurry of shots from Stroud drove Longarm back for a moment, and as he came out into the alley he saw that Stroud had reached the wagon. He was perched on the seat, whipping the team violently as he sent the horses lunging forward. Longarm ran after it and leaped, grabbing the wagon's tailgate with one hand. He hung on for dear life as the vehicle careened around a corner and headed for Buffalo Flat's main street.

The next turn was too much. Longarm couldn't maintain his grip. He went rolling through the mud as the team thundered down the street with Stroud slashing the reins at them madly. Longarm came to a stop on his belly and looked along the street at the racing wagon. He spotted a familiar stocky figure hurrying along the boardwalk beyond the wagon. Marshal Hannibal Gibbs was coming to see what all the shooting was about.

"Stop him!" Longarm shouted to the marshal. "Stop Stroud!"

Gibbs had a shotgun in his hands and could have blown Stroud off the wagon as it went past. But the local lawman hesitated just a second too long, no doubt completely confused by what he was seeing. Stroud's gun blasted again, and Gibbs was rocked back by the slug.

Even as Gibbs fell, however, he finally brought the scattergun into play. The weapon roared as both barrels discharged. The double load of buckshot, fired at close range, shattered several spokes on the wagon's rear wheel. The other spokes couldn't hold up under the strain and snapped. The wheel splintered and came off, dropping the rear corner of the heavily loaded wagon into the mud. It slewed sideways and then came to an abrupt halt, and Charles Stroud was thrown clear of the seat as his own momentum kept him going.

Longarm saw all that as he surged to his feet and ran after the wagon. He wanted to take Stroud alive. He had seen that vault door close on Karen Wilkes and knew that Stroud was the only one who possessed the combination that would free her in time to save her life.

Stroud wasn't going to give up, though. He scrambled to his feet and lunged toward the shelter of the wrecked wagon, firing toward Longarm as he ran. Longarm aimed below the blossoming Colt flame from Stroud's gun and squeezed off a couple of shots, hoping to knock the man's legs out from under him. One of the bullets found its target and Stroud went down, sliding through the mud until half of his body was under the rear corner of the wagon supported by one wheel.

The vehicle's axle must have been cracked in the wreck, because it suddenly split with a sound like a gunshot. The remaining rear wheel, with nothing to brace it, twisted and came off its hub. The back end of the wagon fell . . .

And came down right on Charles Stroud's head.

Longarm grimaced and looked away. He had seen some ugly sights in his career as a lawman, but this was one of the ugliest. The wagon itself was heavy, but with all that money, including bags and bags of gold coins, in it, too . . . well, the result was ugly, and that was all there was to say about it.

Marshal Gibbs was struggling to sit up. Longarm ran over to him, not looking back at what was left of Stroud, and asked, "Are you hit bad, Marshal?"

"Got a damn hole in my leg!" said Gibbs. "Reckon I'll live, though. What the hell's goin' on here?"

"No time for explanations," Longarm said curtly. "Is there any dynamite around here?"

"Might be some at the general store," said Gibbs, his voice taut from the pain of his wound.

"Don't arrest me for breaking in there," Longarm said over his shoulder as he started to run toward the store. Blowing that door off the vault without killing Karen in the process would be tricky, but he had to give it a try.

He kicked the door of the store open, lit a lamp, and

searched swiftly, finding a box of dynamite in the rear storeroom. Gibbs hobbled up, using his shotgun for a crutch, as Longarm emerged from the store. "Damn it, Long—"

More townspeople were showing up, drawn by the shooting and the general commotion. Longarm told a couple of them, "Help the marshal over to the bank." Then he ran across the street and down the alley to the back door. That would be faster than trying to bust in the front.

He found Millie sitting on the floor with Salado's head cradled in her lap. She was crying, but they seemed to be tears of relief. The young man's eyes were open and he was coherent. His right shoulder was covered with blood. It looked like he wasn't going to be using either arm for a while.

Longarm helped Millie lift Salado onto his feet. "You two get out of here," he said as he went to the vault door and took a stick of dynamite from his pocket. It was already capped and fused, ready to light. He wedged it in place against the handle of the vault door and dug a lucifer out of his pocket. A glance over his shoulder told him that Millie and Salado were gone.

"Karen!" he shouted, not knowing whether she could hear him through the thick door. "Get back as far away from the door as you can!"

He flicked the lucifer into life with his thumbnail and held the flame to the end of the fuse.

Then he ducked out through the rear door and ran along the alley for several yards before dropping into a crouch behind a full rain barrel. The blast ripped out from the bank's back room, shaking the muddy ground under Longarm's feet.

He leaped up and ran to the door as Marshal Gibbs and several of the citizens came down the alley, shouting questions. Longarm stepped into the smoke-filled room and waved his hand back and forth in front of his face, clearing away some of the choking smoke. He saw the vault door hanging crooked on its hinges. From the looks of it, there might not be too much damage in the vault itself.

Longarm stepped up to the opening, said, "Karen?" and then stopped short at the sight of the huddled figure lying on the floor at the back of the vault. Grim lines formed trenches in his cheeks. He saw the black-rimmed hole in her temple, the gun lying beside her limp hand. She had already been dead when he blew the door off the vault. She had chosen to take the quick way out, rather than dying slowly from lack of air.

And once again, just as when she had thrown her lot in with Charles Stroud, it had been the wrong decision.

Chapter 20

"Blaze Harker is still right here in Buffalo Flat," said Longarm. "He's buried in the local cemetery under the name Benjamin Stroud."

He was in the front room of Dr. Maxwell's house. Salado Kyle was lying in the bed with his right shoulder now bandaged to match the left. He wouldn't be doing any more gunslinging or poker-playing for a long time. It was when you had two bum wings that you really found out who your friends were, Longarm had told him earlier with a grin. Luckily for Salado, he seemed to have a pretty good friend in Millie.

Marshal Hannibal Gibbs was there, too, his leg bandaged where Stroud had shot him. He sat on a chair with the injured limb stretched out in front of him as he said, "But the bank was open here before that train robbery up in Colorado."

Longarm nodded. "Harker believed in planning ahead. And he figured there wouldn't be any better place to hide a fortune in stolen money than in a bank vault with a bunch of other money. So he started the bank here and established himself as Benjamin Stroud, then went off to rob that train at Cottonwood Station with Gammon and Farley.

He probably told folks he was going to be gone for a couple of weeks on a business trip, or something like that."

"Yeah, that sounds right," mused Gibbs. "I seem to recall him bein' out of town for a little while, not long after the bank opened."

Longarm shook his head. "What's mighty ironic is that the bank was pretty successful on its own. Stroud must've had a talent for finance that went beyond holding up trains. Maybe he didn't intend to stick around Buffalo Flat for as long as he did, but he changed his mind when the bank began to pay off."

"But he still had the loot from the robbery, too."

"Yep, although some of it may have been used just in the course of the banking business. In fact, I'd be surprised if Stroud and then his son didn't slip some of it out into circulation from time to time. When the authorities sent out the information about the stolen bills, it would have come straight to Harker, since he was the only banker in these parts."

"Sounds like he was a mighty tricky son of a bitch," Gibbs commented. "But then he died."

"Hard to be tricky enough to get out of that," said Longarm. "Harker had already brought his son in on the deal, though. Charles just took over and kept going. Nobody knew that fortune in stolen money was anywhere near Buffalo Flat . . . until an old outlaw named Claude Farley happened to see Benjamin Stroud's picture in a newspaper he came across. Even with that shaved head, Farley recognized Stroud as Blaze Harker. He wrote him a letter." Longarm slipped an envelope out of his pocket and handed it to Gibbs. He had found it in Charles Stroud's house as he searched the place while Gibbs and Salado Kyle were having their wounds patched up. "Farley didn't know Harker was already dead. He threatened him, told him that he was coming to Buffalo Flat and expected his share of the money, otherwise he would expose Harker's true identity.

Farley mentioned that he had written to Jasper Gammon, too, and that Harker had better be ready to pay off Gammon as well."

Gibbs snorted. "Hell, that was practically askin' to be bushwhacked! What happened to Farley, anyway?"

Longarm glanced at Millie, who pointedly looked away. "He died of natural causes up in Kansas before he could make the trip down here to Texas to reclaim his share of the loot."

Gibbs looked over at Salado and Millie and asked, "How do you two come into this?"

"They were giving me a hand," Longarm said quickly. "They knew Farley up in Kansas, and when they found out what he was up to, they notified the U.S. Marshal's office. Between that and the help they gave me down here, I'd say that qualifies them for the reward the railroad offered for the Cottonwood Station robbers." Longarm knew he might have to do some fast talking to get Billy Vail to go along with that, but he had a hunch Vail would agree once he heard the whole story.

Gibbs pointed a blunt finger at Salado. "You were shot. How come you to show up at the bank when you did?"

Salado inclined his head toward his left shoulder and explained, "This wound was hurting so much I couldn't sleep. So I was looking out the window when I saw Millie crossing the street with that Wilkes woman. I wasn't sure, but I thought something was wrong."

"Something was wrong, all right," Millie put in. "She had a gun stuck in my ribs. I'm sorry she died—I didn't mean for that to happen when I threw her in that vault and closed the door—but she really was evil."

Salado went on, "I managed to get out of bed without Doc hearing, got my gun, and followed them. It took me a while to get over there, though. I wasn't moving very fast. They were already inside the building, so I had to wait until I was sure what was going on."

"Then you came in to rescue me," said Millie as she perched on the edge of the bed beside him.

Salado looked uncomfortable. "Damn it, don't go making out like I'm some sort of hero," he muttered. "You know good and well I'm not."

Gibbs chuckled and said, "Maybe when you get healed up, you'd be interested in a job, son. I been lookin' for a good deputy, maybe some young fella who could take over as marshal when I hang up my badge in a few years."

Salado stared at him. "Me? A lawman? That's crazy! That's—"

"Something we'll have to think about," Millie said. "Like I was thinking about seeing if the lady who runs the dress shop could use some help."

"I expect she could," said Gibbs with a solemn nod.

Longarm was already edging toward the doorway during this conversation. While Salado was arguing, putting up a valiant defense against encroaching respectability, Longarm slipped out of the office and closed the door quietly behind him. He took a deep breath of the cool night air and then chuckled as he shook his head. He patted his pockets, then remembered that he still hadn't gotten any fresh cheroots.

Hard to believe that only a little over twenty-four hours had passed since he first rode into Buffalo Flat. He had planned to poke around and try to stir up some trouble, just to see what would happen. The plan had worked spectacularly well. The stolen money had been recovered. Of course, it had cost several lives. Longarm wouldn't lose any sleep over Charles Stroud, but he felt a twinge of regret when he thought about Karen Wilkes. He had known her only for a brief period of time and didn't know what had led her to follow the path that had resulted in her death. Questions like that were always hard to answer.

On a more pleasant note, he wondered if there would be a couple of weddings in Buffalo Flat in the near future.

Millie might want to make it legal, and Longarm didn't figure Salado would win that argument, either. And there were still Beth Ferrell and Bob Teague to consider. No telling what would happen with those two.

The only thing certain was that he would be gone before either of those couples said "I do." Somewhere out there, another case was waiting for him, and chances were Billy Vail wouldn't waste any time sending him on his way. That was all right with Longarm. After all these years, he wouldn't know any other way to be.

As long as he had a chance to stock up on those three-for-a-nickel cheroots first . . .

Watch for

**LONGARM AND THE
LITTLE LADY**

the 321st novel in the exciting LONGARM
series from Jove

Coming in August!

J. R. ROBERTS

THE GUNSMITH